Age is a number: keep with going strong!

Gail Cushman
September 2021

Wrinkly Bits

Out of Time

A Wrinkly Bits Senior Hijinks Romance

Gail Decker Cushman

Endorsements

"Cushman's writing in her *Wrinkly Bits* series is fresh, smart, and makes me look forward to a spicier second half of life. Here's to senior romance; it sounds a heck of a lot more fun than twenty-somethings on Tinder."

AK Turner,
New York Times bestselling author of
This Little Piggy Went to the Liquor Store

"*Cruise Time*, the first book in Gail Cushman's *Wrinkly Bits* series, kept me entertained as Audrey Lyon packs her bags—both literally and figuratively— and sets sail with her husband of nearly fifty years. Can they rekindle the spark, or will Audrey spend her time fantasizing about having an affair with a handsome stranger? I highly recommend these books!"

Laurie Buchanan,
author of *Note to Self, The Business of Being,*
and the Sean McPherson suspense/thriller novels.

"Gail Cushman's new book is a delightful comedy and reminds us that romance is not merely for the under 30s. It is both funny and poignant, and I can't wait to read the next volume of her series, *Wrinkly Bits*.

Patricia Werhane,
documentary producer,
BIG QUESTIONS PRODUCTIONS.

"Gail Cushman's *Wrinkly Bits* books are well-written and homey, with delightful tongue-in-cheek story telling. These books were a breath of fresh air."

Chuck Sacrison
Book Reviewer, LTC Retired, U.S. Army

"The refreshing whimsy in these pages is a welcomed perspective as I navigate the season of life where I can hardly fathom doing anything other than chasing around my four little kids and trying to keep up with the general chaos of life. Cushman's capacity for shaping a scene and an experience through words and wit are like a mini vacation—and, filled with heart and tenderness to spark reflection and proper prioritization in life."

Megan Bryant,
Improv Trainer and Award-winning Comedian and Author

"I've often wondered why there are so few books about senior romances. So I was delighted to happen upon Gail Cushman's *Wrinkly Bits* series. These books are clever reminders that much of life actually does begin after 60, when the kids are gone, money has been saved, and bucket lists need attention. I flew through the first two in the series, *Cruise Time* and *Out of Time*, during our last Mediterranean cruise!"

Barbara Jo Charters
Ageless Adventurer and 53-time Cruiser

"I absolutely love being in the midst of a book only to find myself smiling, chuckling, even pausing for the occasional chortle and good old fashioned belly laugh. Gail Cushman's humor shines through *Wrinkly Bits* sharing fun tales of travel through the eyes of adventurous seniors, and it proves to be just what you need to brighten your day. Looking forward to the next books in the series!"

Cindy Turner,
Travel Advisor

"There should be more books out there like this! There is so much of life to be lived and Gail Cushman's *Wrinkly Bits* series made me laugh and think there is so much adventure ahead in our lives, we just have to be willing. Cushman's books are easy to read and highly entertaining."

Lori Hosac,
Sales Manager

"Since retiring I have had more time to read and have looked forward to Gail Cushman's blog *Wrinkly Bits*. So I was happy to learn of her series of books with the same title. Their light-hearted nature is especially welcome during the challenging times we all are experiencing now."

Jim Mitchell
Owner Jim's IGA, Mitchell's IGA,
and D9 IGA in Idaho.

Edited by AnnaMarie McHargue and Anita Stephens
Designed by Leslie Hertling

www.wrinklybits.com

Dedicated to
Elizabeth Cushman Hume
and
Cole Cushman

(You know why!)

CHAPTER 1
Griff

Audrey clicked off the phone with Phyllis and announced to her husband, "Good news, Griff, we're going to a party. Phyllis and Gus are throwing some big shindig next week. She called it an EJL party, End of Jet Lag, you know Phyllis and her text talking. The whole gang's coming, and it should be fun."

"I could use a party," Griff responded, "being house-bound in a wheelchair is no picnic in the woods, and I'm ready to rock and roll." Griff punctuated his comments with a couple of fist pumps and said, "Chugga, chugga. Maybe we can do some dancing and even better, you and I can do some sheet shakin', you know some three-a-days, like we used to." Griff, now age seventy and retired, had discovered SXTV and the little blue pill and had delusions that he was eighteen, wanting to *do the dirty* three times a day. Audrey at age sixty-seven was less enthusiastic.

A sixsome of retirees from Hunter, Idaho, had recently returned from a two-week-long repositioning cruise from Fort Lauderdale to Lisbon and enjoyed it thoroughly. They added friendships with two more, both physicians, who ended up in Hunter, too. Everyone except Dr. Lewis was over sixty, with an average age of sixty-eight, and they rattled around the ship as if they were kids again. The trip served as an elixir to add a spring to their steps and joy to their hum-drum world.

The whole gang included not only Griff and Audrey, but also retired dentist Steve Sanderson and his wife, Carlee, who successfully practiced alcoholism. Gus and Phyllis Gustafson were the third couple;

they had retired from teaching a few years earlier, became cruisaholics, and enjoyed a couple of trips each year. Phyllis craved adventure and constantly watched for new and adventurous things, and it became her mantra. Joining the Hunter travelers were Doctors Logan Hall and Vivian Lewis, both of whom had been welcomed into the group. Audrey had welcomed Logan, and Gus had welcomed Dr. Lewis.

Griff had retired from farming soybeans and hops, and Audrey had retired as an LPN at a local chemical dependency treatment center. Griff liked to fish and hunt, and *do the dirty*, although his desire and his ability didn't exactly match without the help of modern chemistry.

Logan Hall, from Portland, Oregon, was a retired podiatrist and widower, and Audrey, without knowing it, had knocked him off his socks. His palms and forehead dripped whenever she was near. With similar interests of health and exercise, they became inseparable, almost a twosome, but no one knew the extent of their relationship. Phyllis suggested that they were BFFs, best friends forever, but the others wondered if they had moved it up a notch, to FWB, friends with benefits, whatever those benefits might be. Dr. Vivian Lewis, the ship's doctor, had helped Gus through panic attacks, and fully dedicated herself to Gus' recuperation. She became involved in daily rehab sessions, which she called calibrations, sometimes lasting an hour or more.

"No chugga, chugga today, Griff, you have to be able to walk and do normal things," Audrey replied. "By the way, Phyllis asked that we bring some hors d'oeuvres to share, and I'd like to use up those fish you caught last summer. I can make fish sticks for an appetizer, but the trout are frozen, and our kitchen drain is clogged. It's dirty and nasty, and I can't thaw the fish in the sink until it's fixed. I need to call a plumber; do you know anyone?"

"I can fix the drain, Hon, if you help me," Griff scowled emphatically. "We don't need to spend money on something I can do." Griff and Audrey had worked hard for their money and had watched every penny they earned. They had both retired a couple years prior and sold their farm for more than they had anticipated, but old habits die hard, and they continued pinching pennies, although Griff pinched harder than Audrey.

"You're in a wheelchair, Griff, and what about your knee and your back? And your bunion? I'll find somebody. I'll call Rosemary Sage, and maybe her son would help us. He's handy and won't charge us much, plus I think he could use the extra money."

After he had retired, Griff had developed an oversized and sensitive bunion that podiatrist Logan Hall splinted while traveling to Lisbon. On the final night of the cruise, the toe splint, coupled with a little too much demon rum, caused him to fall off his knee scooter, injuring his knee and wrenching his back. The ship's doctor confined him to a wheelchair and he still wore the toe splint. In addition, his knee hurt and back twitched, so he continued using the wheelchair as he moved throughout the house. Over-the-counter pain medicine didn't help, and he had refused to visit his primary care physician. Logan had wrapped the injuries and suggested physical therapy, but Griff resisted. Between his height, the extra girth he earned while cruise dining, and his injuries, he had become dependent on the chair.

"You figure it out, I've gotta take care of business," Griff growled, aiming the wheelchair toward the bathroom.

"Griff, don't forget to shower," Audrey called after him. "You've worn that flannel shirt for three days, and it has spots on it, and it smells. Toss it in the dirty clothes basket, and I'll bring you another."

He shouted back, "We could shower together, you know SWB, showers with benefits," he called back, "like FWB, friends with benefits that Phyllis keeps mentioning. You could wash my back and I could wash your front, and we'd be done in no time. What do you think?"

"No dice until you're out of that wheelchair. No SWB or FWB till you get well," she returned, asking herself if she would have agreed to a SWB with Logan. Maybe.

"All right," Griff grumbled, unbuttoning the shirt and sliding it from his chest. "Where's the dirty clothes basket? It isn't here." He was sitting on the toilet and tossed the shirt over his shoulder toward the toilet tank, where it immediately burst into flames from the scented candle Audrey had placed on the back of the toilet.

Audrey stepped to the bathroom and tossed him a different plaid shirt, "Wear this one, it's clean. No, no! Griff, it's on fire!" She grabbed a towel from the rack and fanned the flames, which escalated into a real fire and caught another towel on fire.

Griff shouted, "Don't fan them, Audrey, cover them with something and throw on a wet towel. He leaned forward on the toilet to move out of her way and lost his balance, crashing face-first to the floor. He hit his head and went quiet.

"Griff, are you okay? Can you stand or sit?" He was lying face down on the floor in the bathroom doorway, naked, except for his toe splint. Blood trickled from his nose and forehead. She dipped a towel in the sink and tossed it on the expanding flames, extinguishing them immediately.

His nose now oozed blood, and he didn't answer immediately, then, "Just give me a minute," he squeaked, "and maybe a hand." He tried to boost himself up on his forearms but couldn't put weight on his injured knee and collapsed back to the floor. His back began to spasm as he tried with little progress to inch out of the doorway.

Audrey gave him a wet towel for his facial cuts and tossed a bath sheet across his back saying, "I'll call 911, they can help you."

"No, that'll...money...and I can do it. Not a baby," Griff stammered, continuing, "left foot hurts...broken," and he passed out.

CHAPTER 2
Phyllis

Phyllis Gustafson had set her sights on doing something fun. Two weeks of jet lag weighed heavy, especially with Gus' health issues. He had suffered a panic attack while on the cruise and she, along with Dr. Vivian Lewis, had been nursing him back to health. "Way to go, Gus, Darling, I'm so proud of you. You did two flights of stairs this morning. You were weak and infirm on the cruise and didn't improve much on the way home, I was scared you would die, but look at you! You're on a roll. Two flights of stairs, alone, without Dr. Lewis' or my help. Let's whoop it up! Let's have a party!"

Both Gus and Phyllis retired four years ago from teaching high school after having taught a cajillion kids, most of whom they enjoyed, although they could both name a few they didn't, mostly the same kids, but that's another story. Gus earned the label Mr. Physical Fitness, coaching everything from football to cheerleading, and Phyllis had struggled watching his physical health deteriorate during the last few years, although the reason lay front and center, especially front, meaning his expanding belly.

When he retired, he wanted to play golf and watch TV, preferably shows with *babes* and wore a clear path in the carpet between his chair and the refrigerator. He used to laugh and say, *that's why they have commercials* (he called them snack-attacks). And now, he floated the dial on the bathroom scale to over three hundred pounds with a plethora of ailments, only a few diagnosed, and because he thought he was tough, he was reluctant to see his physician, meaning his actual diagnoses ran thin.

Life had crashed down on Gus, and Phyllis feared she would lose him, but the ship's doctor, Dr. Lewis, gave him an ultimatum: change his lifestyle, or he could take a permanent nap on the big hammock in the sky. One who disliked doctors, Gus became fond of her and listened, becoming the first person ever to lose weight on a cruise. Through Dr. Lewis' calibration technique, he watched his diet, began moving more, a little, not too much, and his weight plunged a full thirty pounds. Her suggestions of no booze, no whoopy, reduced portions, and increased exercise made for a rather dreary two weeks, but as far as anyone knew, he hadn't given into booze, and of course, he and Phyllis avoided dancing the horizontal hula.

"I'm finally over jet lag. I can't recall ever feeling so tired after a cruise," Phyllis commented to Gus, speculating whether jet lag, the cruise, or extra-curricular activities caused her fatigue. She had two adventures on the trip, although she had made a good attempt for three, but Gus wasn't aware of any.

Gus wholeheartedly agreed, "That sounds fine, let's invite the whole gang. I'd enjoy seeing them all. This Idaho cold snap has made our life miserable and it's time to have a little fun. Invite everybody including Dr. Lewis and Logan," Gus directed. "Are they both staying at the Hunter Inn? Let's make it a good party, food, wine, and music, and we can ask everyone to bring something."

Phyllis eagerly agreed, "I'll start calling everybody this morning and am going to plan it for next weekend. That will give you a little more time to gain some strength. When we all are together, we can talk about our next trip. You need to throw the dart again, but make it land someplace new. Griff's already thinking about Aruba with beaches and bikinis, Audrey's thinking of a tour of France. Carlee votes for France, but she's not interested in Versailles, as she obviously would rather tour the vineyards, and I am anxious to acquire charms for my new bracelet, so I'm open to whatever our next adventure brings. I hope Logan and Dr. Lewis will be able to join us on our next cruise because it wouldn't be the same without them." Her lower girl parts did a happy dance as she thought of Griff and Steve who had made the transatlantic trip oh-so interesting. Logan appealed to her, but his appetite for Audrey had forced her to put him on hold, but another trip meant another opportunity.

Steve, age seventy-eight, the most senior of the group, had practiced dentistry in Salt Lake City, but after retirement he and Carlee moved to Hunter to be near their children and for its more tranquil atmosphere. Sexy and amusing, Carlee, who had recently turned sixty, owned a healthy appetite for all things sexual. Her body resembled that of a fit thirty-year-old, but her tanned and wrinkled skin mirrored crepe paper.

The vacation to Lisbon had been fraught with adventure. Gus and Phyllis were cruisaholics, Steve and Carlee loved the sea, but it was an inaugural cruise for Audrey and Griff, who had found fun and frolic in all kinds of new escapades. Logan had spiced things up for everyone, especially Audrey, and Dr. Lewis drew in Gus.

People who cruise often collect things, from postcards to t-shirts to thimbles, and Phyllis collected charms for her charm bracelet. Her students had presented her with a sterling silver charm bracelet when she retired and suggested she fill it with remembrances of new adventures. She began collecting on their first cruise to Jamaica, where she met Juan, and realized the possibilities for filling her bracelet were as limitless as were men on cruise ships. She found that she loved to commemorate her adventures and became an enthusiastic and effective collector. On the repositioning cruise to Lisbon, she had been on target to earn a trifecta, but hadn't quite reached it before she tragically lost her bracelet and now needed to restart her collection.

CHAPTER 3
Phyllis

The next morning, Phyllis arose early, excited at the prospect of a party. She created a mental list of things to prepare for a houseful of guests and began to say them aloud, "I've gotta call the crew. If everybody comes, we'll have six guests, plus us, and I'll have to decide about food and drink. I'll call the grocery store and find out if I can order eight live lobsters. I've never cooked them before, but everyone loved lobster night on the ship. How hard can it be to plop them in boiling water?"

"Lobsters will be expensive, but we can do it," Gus agreed. "If I weren't under Dr. Lewis' confounded clutches, I'd have two, maybe three, but I'll stick to one. No butter. We can ask the others to bring something, and I suggest that Logan brings the wine. He knows the best wines and probably won't spare any expense trying to impress Audrey. That'll cut our costs."

"Remember, I'm inviting Dr. Lewis, too, so she'll be watching you, mister," Phyllis reminded him. "She's liable to slap you silly if she thinks you're ignoring her orders. I'll ask her to bring wine, too." Gus had never respected female doctors, but Dr. Lewis struck a chord with her plain, folksy talk, and he listened to her.

As the ship's doctor, she initially treated Gus for a panic attack, which resembled a minor heart attack, and she convinced him to take on a new lifestyle. Her contract with the cruise line had expired, and she explained she wanted to spread her wings. Gus had suggested she come to Hunter, so here she was, now a member of Hunter Hospital's emergency room staff. Podiatrist Logan Hall had also returned with the group to Hunter, mostly due to his budding relationship with Audrey, Phyllis and Carlee thought. They thought his desire was to glide into something more permanent and had now spent two weeks at the local hotel, calling her daily, but unsuccessfully arranging time with her. Griff wasn't happy about Logan's attention to Audrey, but on the other foot, as Logan said, he had splinted his bunion and not charged him anything, so Griff didn't complain about it. Between taking care of Griff and the cold and inclement weather, Audrey had difficulty stealing time to be with Logan, although he was on her mind constantly.

Phyllis finished planning the menu and, while the lobsters were bound to be expensive, Gus remained adamant, insisting they could manage. The planned menu, besides the lobster, was salad, baked potatoes (this was Idaho for crying out loud), appetizers, and dessert. And of course, wine.

Phyllis called Audrey, who was excited, and offered to make fish sticks from the trout Griff had caught recently, and Carlee offered to bring wine, two bottles. Gus could pop potatoes in the oven, and Phyllis would make a green salad. Good to go.

CHAPTER 4
Phyllis

Gus and Phyllis had been in love for forty years and continued to enjoy their mutual flirting, teasing, and romancing. Both big-boned and anorexia free, Gus joked that they offered each other more to love. Phyllis adored Gus and he was crazy for her.

They met and fell in love during their college years. She was an academic type, even a nerd, and gained academic honors, while Gus built a rugged physique with bulging muscles. As a sophomore, Phyllis was selected college homecoming queen, and as a junior, named *who-you-would-most-enjoy-being-trapped-on-a-desert-island-with*. Gus was named *Mr. Magnificent* four years running, based on his physique and handsome face. Their primary dating gigs included weekly fraternity or sorority dances where they won a basketful of prizes. When Phyllis finally said *I do*, Gus said *I don't* to dancing, and they never danced together as a couple again. Phyllis didn't let that stop her and found plenty of dance partners through the years.

They loved teaching and were popular among students and parents. Phyllis, more charismatic than Gus, taught him the art of making every person believe they were the most important one in the room. People told her that she was pretty, but she thought they were shining her on. She had the ability to recall names and bits of information about people, which made them feel important. Her sense of humor created more charisma and she could tell a joke like none other. Her penchant for self-deprecating humor was what people loved and remembered.

They both enjoyed cooking and eating, and Phyllis found it easy to make fun of herself as she doubled her formerly slim and trim twenty-year-old figure. Gus didn't care and said she had created two people for him to love.

Gus coached all boys' sports, baseball, basketball, football, plus volleyball for girls, which made for long days as the volleyball and football seasons ran simultaneously. He developed charisma through his coaching. He, too, had a hearty appetite, and as his weight increased, so did the subsequent health issues that accompany overeating.

As Gus' health declined, Phyllis was determined to help him reduce his Buddhah belly and began trying to shed a few excess pounds of her own. She became a yo-yo dieter, finally giving up, but continued to urge her honeybunch to eat healthier. Retirement and cruising brought even more challenges, but they shrugged it off as being in the *genes*. Phyllis joked that they should have spelled it *j-e-a-n-s*, as none fit.

When they first married, they were determined to have children, but Phyllis had endometriosis and could not bear children. Adoption was expensive, not covered by their health policy, and they decided against it. They agreed to simply adopt the kids in their classrooms, giving them more children than they could ever have on their own. It was Phyllis' idea, but Gus agreed. They saw other people's kids for six hours a day, without the strings of puberty or teenage driving, and could focus on loving each other at night. It was a win-win situation. They involved themselves with school activities and helped lots of kids through difficult times.

Despite their forty years of marriage, they viewed retirement differently. Gus regarded retirement as graduation, leaving work and schedules far behind. Gus' *bucket list* included spending his leisure years with a fishing pole or golf club in his hand, or perhaps doing nothing at all. As a coach, he compared his working career to a basketball game. When the buzzer sounded in the fourth quarter, it was time to go home. No overtime, just time for a beer. He considered retirement the reward for finishing a long and sometimes tedious career of dealing with kids, parents, and sports. He joined a golf league and played a few rounds each week and drank a little beer with his friends. He excelled at both.

Phyllis looked at her retirement in the opposite way, perceiving it as a commencement, starting her life anew, fresh and exciting, like a play. Act I was the teaching part and Act II was retirement, a fresh beginning, with new adventures that would allow her to expand herself beyond Hunter, see the world, and figure out what she had missed all these years.

When her students presented her with a sterling silver charm bracelet and suggested that she fill it with remembrances of traveling the world, finding exhilarating experiences, she thought it was a darned good idea. She developed her *bucket list* with only one item: *new and adventurous things every single day.*

When many of their teaching friends retired, they shut down, drew their pensions and having been actively involved with teaching and after-school events for twenty or thirty years, sat back and did nothing, stayed home, glad to put their feet up and read a book. They played golf or cards or tended a garden and enjoyed it, but before long, loneliness and isolation set in, making every day a clone of Bill Murray's movie *Ground Hog Day*, exactly the same as the day before. Before long, they only discussed their many illnesses, how many pills they ingested, and which doctor would prescribe more. Phyllis determined that Gus and she would not fall into that trap. She thought of herself as a butterfly exiting a cocoon, and within a few weeks, she convinced Gus that cruising would fill her bucket. He asked if the ship would have babes and beer, and when she said yes, he agreed. He continued to watch for babes, but finding none, instead guzzled plenty of beer. Not many babes booked old fogey cruises, but the beer was plentiful.

Soon, they called themselves cruisaholics, traveling throughout the world and Phyllis began acquiring charms for her bracelet to recall all the new places and people they encountered. She had accumulated over twenty charms, each of which made her smile. The tragic loss of her bangle gave her reason to start over. New beginnings could be fun.

Before retiring, they had not traveled much and didn't know

where to start, so during their first year of retirement they bought an oversized map of the world and a dart, and Gus tossed the dart at the map. Wherever the dart landed, they would go, and they had visited much of Mexico, the Caribbean (several times), and Australia, gaining New Zealand and Fiji on the same trip. One time, the dart landed on Venezuela, which happened to be in the middle of a major political upheaval, so they swapped Venezuela for Venice. Both started with *Ven*, they reasoned, and they cruised around Italy, which they believed a logical and safe substitution. Last year, the dart landed on the Aleutians, but their trip would be in October, so they swapped out Alaska for Hawaii where they renewed their wedding vows. This year, the dart hit the Atlantic Ocean, and they found a cruise to the Canary Islands and Lisbon.

"I called the whole crew and invited them to our party, and it looks like everyone's on board. Carlee offered to bring wine, two bottles. We'll do lobsters and baked spuds and a salad. Easy peasy," Phyllis explained to Gus.

Gus said, "Carlee should bring three bottles because she will drink two, and the rest of us could share the third. I know she drinks too much and becomes a little risqué, but she makes me laugh. She's not as witty as you are, though." He enjoyed Carlee's risqué chatter, like when she talked about men's fricks and fracks or her chestnuts. Everyone knew she was talking about sex organs, but she never used the words. It was like code, and people laughed at her bold bawdiness.

"How about Logan and Dr. Lewis? Are they going to come?" Gus asked. "It wouldn't be a reunion without them."

Phyllis responded, "I haven't been able to reach Logan, but I'm sure he'll come. He doesn't seem to be able to take his eyes off Audrey, and if she's here, he won't miss it. I can't help but believe he and Audrey are up to something, but Audrey insists they are just BFFs. Griff hasn't gotten out of the wheelchair, but the party isn't until next week, so he should be better. And I'll talk to Dr. Lewis when she shows up to calibrate you. She hasn't missed a day yet, so I expect she'll come this afternoon."

Dr. Lewis had been treating Gus for about three weeks with something she called a calibration system, keeping track of his health and exercise. Phyllis didn't know exactly what a calibration system was, but Dr. Lewis assured her that she had used it before. She engaged a few medical-type words that brought comfort. Phyllis wanted to see how her system worked, but Dr. Lewis closed and locked the bedroom door while she and Gus calibrated, insisting on no interruptions. Phyllis wondered at the necessity of a daily regimen, but Dr. Lewis was firm, and Gus didn't argue, and if he was happy, Phyllis was happy. His weight had dropped, and he could climb two flights of stairs. His mental attitude seemed more positive, and she hoped that they would be able to get back to their horizontal hula one of these days. He wasn't so keen on dancing on the dance floor, but they used to dance between the sheets often. With a decrease in his poundage and an increase in his agility, Phyllis hoped they would be going strong again sometime very soon.

CHAPTER 5
Carlee

On the first day back from the cruise, Carlee and Steve drove to the post office to retrieve their mail, which was bundled and ready.

"Did you have a good trip, Carlee?" the postal worker asked. "Phyllis came in earlier today talking about some sleigh ride that you took. I didn't know you went to snow country; I thought it was the Mediterranean."

"We went to Portugal, which was warm, at least compared to Hunter. Steve and I didn't take the sled ride, but everyone else did and they said it was fun. Steve and I did a little shopping that day, testing out the Portuguese wine. Did a package come for us?" Carlee inquired.

"No, no packages, the usual: bills, ads, and offers for free stuff, the same as I receive."

Steve rifled through the mail noticing, "Junk mail, of course. I was hoping the hotel had sent my hearing aids. I told the hotel guy to mail them back, and you would think that three weeks would be plenty of time for them to arrive. Would you call the hotel to find out where the hell they are? I'd call but I won't be able to hear or decipher anything they say."

Carlee ramped up her cell phone and thumbed through her *previous calls* list, trying to remember which number was the Ritzy-Que hotel in Fort Lauderdale. She had called several places on the day they departed for the cruise, but she hadn't bothered to record any of them, meaning she had a long list of numbers from which to choose. She punched in six sets of numbers before she reached the Ritzy-Que where they had stayed the night before the cruise.

"Lila speaking," the voice on the other end of the phone said, "How can I help you?"

"Lila, I'm Carlee Sanderson from Idaho. We stayed at your hotel a few weeks ago and my husband left his hearing aids in the room. Could you tell us whether you mailed them to us? The room was registered under the name of Steve Sanderson." She spoke slowly and clearly as she had talked with Lila before.

Lila perked up, "Oh, yes, I remember you. My manager took them to the pier, but the ship was leaving just as he arrived. Bummer. I don't know what he did with them because he quit the Ritzy-Que the next day and now has a different job. I don't know where he is or how to reach him. He might have moved to Miami."

"Oh, frack, maybe he left them in his office or something? Lila, could you check? I suppose you don't have a phone number you can share either?" Carlee said.

"I can't give out his cell number because that's personal information, but I'll ask the new manager to give you a call when he returns from training," Lila said.

"Okay, that'll work," Carlee muttered. "What time does he finish his training? It's a two-hour time difference and I don't want to miss his call."

"I don't know. Manager training lasts longer than desk clerk training, so it might be a few days," Lila answered.

CHAPTER 6
Dr. Lewis

Audrey called 911. Griff had done a face plant and stunned himself and lay silent on the floor without moving for several seconds before he began to shift his body and complain. He was breathing so she waited, hoping the EMTs would hurry. They lived eighteen miles out of town, and even in good weather, it wasn't a quick trip.

Griff's nose dripped blood, and she applied an icepack, which made him chilly, so she replaced the bath sheet with a blanket and moved a space heater into the bathroom. She didn't think his foot was broken but couldn't be sure without an X-ray. She could tell he was in pain and generally miserable. He moaned and whimpered unintelligibly, and Audrey began to massage his back and plugged in their ancient heating pad. He opened his eyes, sighed, and closed them again. He growled at her asking why she chose today to put a candle in the bathroom, and what was the matter with her.

Winter ruts on unpaved roads and mounds of dirty snow slowed the arrival of emergency services for an hour until they pulled into the Lyons' driveway. Two EMTs and four firemen waded through the slush, toting slings, back boards, and a gurney to transport Griff. He had regained consciousness but moved in slow motion as they slapped him into a sling and whisked him to the ambulance. Sniffing the pungent fumes from the burned shirt and towel, the firemen verified that the fire was out, but it had scorched both the towel and shirt rendering both unsalvageable.

Audrey decided to ride with Griff and the EMTs to Hunter Hospital and hitch a ride back to the farm after Griff had been seen. She knew she could ask Logan to bring her home, in fact, he would insist. She popped her ancient flip phone into her purse and donned a coat, gloves, and a scarf for the journey to town. The ambulance contained a portable X-ray machine that confirmed that Griff had cracked his fibula, and the EMTs offered him pain pills, which he eagerly accepted. The injured knee and toe splint were on his left side and the fibula break was on the right. The loss of consciousness worried her, although he was alert now.

Audrey didn't know if the Hunter Hospital had an orthopedic surgeon on staff, but if it did, she didn't know his or her name. Griff wasn't fond of Logan, but Audrey trusted him and hoped Griff would appreciate Logan's extra attention. She called Logan as soon as they arrived at the hospital. The sound of his voice caused her to suck in and hold her breath and floated her girl juices to the surface, and she began to babble as she often did in his presence.

"Logan, can you come to the hospital? Griff broke his foot, and we're in the ER," Audrey said.

"He broke his foot? Which one?" Logan asked.

"The one in Hunter," Audrey responded quickly. "Going to Pocatello will take too long."

"No, not which hospital, which bone?" Logan asked patiently.

"The right foot, Logan, but what difference does it make?" Audrey said, annoyed at his lack of comprehension.

"No, I don't mean which foot, which bone?" Logan repeated.

"I don't know, a foot bone. They said *his foot bone.* That's all. How many bones does the foot have?"

"Well, a lot actually, twenty-six bones and thirty-three joints, all of which are breakable. His feet are not quite as sexy as yours are, but he most likely has the same number of bones and joints," Logan flirted.

Audrey's awkwardness continued, and she found herself annoyed that she felt turned on when she should have been worried about Griff. Her face and chest heated up with a warm glow that crept through her body, and she barely listened to what Logan was saying. "That many? I suppose most bones are in the toes, right?"

Logan continued, "Did he break the toe with the bunion? Does he need a new toe splint?"

"No, he broke the other foot. His knee issue and bunion are on the left, and the break is on the right. He lost consciousness, too, but now he's as mad as a chicken in the rain. He's a mess," Audrey commented, as she continued to heat up, thirsting for a glass of water.

Logan said, "I'll come by in a few minutes. I don't have hospital privileges, but I can give moral support. I'll bring another toe splint, too, because that one is probably caput."

CHAPTER 7
Dr. Lewis

"**O**h, my gosh, it's you, Dr. Lewis. Phyllis mentioned that you worked here, but I didn't expect to see you. Look, Griff, it's Dr. Lewis from the ship." The two women hugged each other, and Audrey said, "Griff needs help, he set his shirt on fire and fell off the toilet this morning, and he blacked out for a minute or two."

Dr. Lewis brightened, "Hi, Griff, honey. You already hurt your toe, knee, and back and now your foot? You're like that old rhyme: head, shoulders, knees, and toes, except you don't have an injured shoulder. Yet. And it is your nose in addition to your head, back, knee, toe, and foot although the toe splint is working for you. EMTs tell me you bumped your head. Your entire lower half is a mess, and your nose is quite the sight to lay eyes on, too." She picked up a damp cloth and began swabbing the oozes of blood from his face.

Dr. Lewis had attended a premium medical school and graduated second in her class. She was reared in rural Nevada by a single mom who struggled to put food on the table for her brood of seven children. The youngest child, Vivian, later Dr. Vivian Lewis, aspired to become a veterinarian but found it easier to be accepted into medical school, so she applied for and received multiple scholarships, and her six older siblings paid the rest of the bill.

As a teenager, she puzzled about forbidden fruit, and questioned why her mother had chosen the four now-absent men in her life that had fathered her seven children. What was the appeal? Her curiosity led to her investigating the human libido and became fascinated with its licit and illicit incongruities. Medical school did not offer libido classes; indeed, they would have been popular, but she sought out a few focus groups that helped identify and explain the many unanswered whys and why nots of modern and ancient medical issues, including sex and love.

Smart and sassy, she graduated ahead of most her classmates and spent time in rural clinics where she encountered a good variety of experiences, but rural communities began to bore her. Small towns offered few dating opportunities and the available men did not live up to her standards. After a few years and innumerable unsuccessful romances, she looked at travel opportunities to expand her life beyond treating snotty noses and nausea. She finally settled on the idea of working on a cruise line, applied, was hired, and had been sailing the seas for six years before she met the group from Hunter, Idaho. She had known, in the Biblical sense, several men through the years, but when she met Gus, God knows why, he whistled her dixie, and she made up her mind: forbidden fruit or not, she didn't want to lose him. Gus was married to Phyllis and she knew they loved each other, but he was irresistible. She thought of him as her soulmate, her dreamboat. Phyllis called him *her everything,* but Gus was man enough for the both of them.

The EMTs passed the X-ray to Dr. Lewis, and she said, "You managed to crack your fibula, my dear Griff, and now this baby's swollen like a pregnant watermelon, so we'll ice it and splint it until the swelling recedes before we cast it. And your left knee looks swollen, too. Did you bang it again when you fell off the toilet? What about your head?" She flickered a flashlight in front of his eyes and asked him some questions, but he insisted he was fine. "You're actually a mess from your eyebrows down, but I'll fix you up."

The pills the EMTs had given Griff lowered his pain, but they also changed his mindset from whininess to irascibility and he became a combination of bullheaded, argumentative, and cantankerous. He threw out a litany of accusations toward Audrey regarding the bathroom candle and Logan about the bunion, "Yes, the bunion hasn't gone completely away, and I have trouble wearing my shoes. I've had nothing but trouble since *Doctor* Logan Hall splinted it," Griff used his hands to indicate quotation marks around *doctor*. "I was doing fine until the toe quack tried to treat me, and now, I have serious problems. And I haven't even seen a doctor about my kidney stones or my macular degeneration." Griff glanced over at Audrey and shot her a warning stink-eye. "I haven't complained about it much, but I'm sure I have both, and I need them fixed or, at least, you should tell me what's wrong."

"I didn't know…" Audrey's voice trailed off as the stink-eye thumped her face.

Griff was on a roll and interrupted her, "Yeah, well, hell, Audrey, I didn't tell you because I didn't want to worry you. Also, Doc, I'm out of those blue pills, so can you prescribe some more of those? Audrey and I have a hot date, don't we, Hon, as soon as you fix these other things."

Doctor Lewis twisted her mouth and raised her eyebrows, wondering at this strange conversation. Maybe he had suffered a head injury, something to note. "Macular degeneration and ED are not emergency room diagnostic arenas, but I'll take a look at those kidney stones," she informed Griff, as she exited the room.

Griff could be cantankerous, but he was worse than usual, and Audrey thought the drugs might be messing with his brain. He whispered, "Play along, Audrey, if we can have her take care of all these, we won't have to see another doctor and pay more deductible and co-pays. I'm trying to save us some money. We spent a fortune on the cruise, and we need to pull it back."

"Do you think you have kidney stones?" Audrey asked incredulously. "Do you have abdominal pain? You haven't mentioned it, and kidney stones are painful."

"I don't know yet, but I might soon. I don't have any pain, but Steve told me he had them when he was my age, and it might be an age thing. The doc can check, and it'll be the same price."

CHAPTER 8
Griff

Dr. Logan Hall arrived at the hospital, a new toe splint in tow. Griff's eyes lay closed, and he appeared to be sleeping, so he greeted Audrey with a peck on the cheek, sliding his hand across her derriere, shielding the act from her husband. She shrieked a tiny sound and gave out a shiver as her eyes went wide and glistened. Griff rallied full bore at the sight of Logan kissing his wife on the cheek. "Logan, cut that out," Griff roared in his surliest manner, "she's my wife."

"That's true, but we are friends, perhaps even BFFs," he smiled first at Audrey, then at Griff, before examining Griff's bunion and observed aloud that it had diminished in size and color. He poked and prodded and asked Griff a few questions and announced that the bunion was doing nicely, and Griff could forego the splint for the time being.

Dr. Lewis burst into the room and poured out information, "Griff, we are going to keep you in the hospital for at least one night. You sound a little off your game and a little goofy, and I wonder if you injured your head a bit. I don't want you to risk a little fall or injuring yourself worse, or falling on Audrey. If the swelling subsides, we can cast it tomorrow, and you can go home on crutches or the wheelchair tomorrow night. If not tomorrow, the next day, unless something else happens. It's cracked, not broken, and it should heal nicely in a week or two. As for the kidney stones, you don't appear to have abdominal pain, so you should see your regular doctor for that exam, and Dr. Hall seems in charge of the bunion. Does that work for you, Dr. Hall?"

"So how about the blue…" Griff's voice trailed off as his eyes crossed to Logan. It would not do at all if Logan thought he relied on the blue pill for his three-a-days with Audrey.

"Nope, sorry, primary physician," Dr. Lewis chuckled, adding, "You'll have to wait a few days before you shift into that business again." She looked at Audrey, noting her flushed face that had transformed from tense to relaxed since Logan arrived.

Dr. Lewis gave Griff a sleeping pill causing him to doze off within minutes. While the staff transferred him to a hospital room on the third floor, she said, "You look like you could use a break, Audrey, and Griff's going to be asleep for a while. We can call you when he wakes up. You can't do anything to help so you two should enjoy a nice lunch while he's resting. Maybe you and Logan would like to have some alone time, too." She, too, had suspected they were more than BFFs. She nudged Audrey with her elbow, "If you know what I mean."

"That's a splendid idea," Logan answered without hesitation. "I'd love to take Miss Audrey to lunch or maybe ice cream."

"Thank you, Dr. Lewis, I could use a break and some food. I hadn't yet eaten breakfast when we had to come to town, and I'm on the verge of starvation. The hospital cafeteria is shut down for cleaning and besides one bar that probably isn't open this early, there aren't many eating establishments close to the hospital."

"My hotel has a good restaurant, and it's close. We can walk," Logan said.

"Before we go, could I ask you a question, Dr. Lewis. I'm curious as to why you decided to stay in Hunter. It's a dinky town with not much entertainment," Audrey commented.

Dr. Lewis nodded, "That's a good question, Audrey, but perhaps the same reason Dr. Logan is staying here." Her eyes twinkled, and she arched her eyebrows, "if you know what I mean." It seemed to be a favorite phrase. "I enjoyed meeting the six of you, seven with Logan, eight and a pooch if we add Mel and Jack Black. Gus was, still is, ill, and needs more attention than Phyllis, bless her heart, is capable of giving him. My mama told me to take care of the special cases specially, and that's what I am doing with Gus. He is my special case, as Phyllis says, *my everything*. I don't know what magic made him special, but whatever it was, he is, and I wouldn't feel right leaving his care to someone else."

CHAPTER 9
Logan

D r. Logan Hall and Audrey met on their cruise to Lisbon and although neither was looking for a tryst, they became smitten as teenagers and soon were inseparable. It was a love-at-first-sight situation, although neither of them believed in the concept. Audrey and Griff inched toward fifty years together, and she had lost her desire for sex, but her normally arid lower deck suddenly developed a lusty vitality that tingled whenever Logan came to mind, which was often. And Logan, a widower of four years, had not had an erection since his wife Joan died, but now his unsuppressed libido raised his flag high and firm every time Audrey came into view or even bounced into his mind. Although he lived in Portland, four hundred miles from Hunter, he had remained in Hunter, desiring to build a relationship with Audrey. He had high hopes of winning her over, although she saw the situation as hopeless. The optimist and the pessimist. In his smitten state, he couldn't bring himself to leave the one person who returned zest to his life. She felt the same, but she was married to Griff.

At age seventy, Logan continued to attract women, and on his previous cruises he seldom dined alone. Women bought him drinks, asked him to dance, and one woman that he had never seen before asked him to marry her. Handsome, charming, funny, and intelligent, any of which attracted women who hoped to link up with someone better than their last husband, he was sought after, but night after night he returned to his cabin alone, never finding another woman to cross the threshold with him. Until Audrey, she was different.

Something drew him to her, and he didn't know what it was or how to handle it. Was it love? Or maybe just sex? But sex had been low on his list after his wife Joan had developed complications from diabetes, which took her life four years ago. Audrey stirred up his libido like crazy, but he had done without sex all this time. So, why Audrey, why now? Plenty of fish-ettes swam on that cruise ship, several of whom made obvious advances, but it was Audrey who had set him aglow.

The problem was Griff. If Griff were not in the picture, he would woo the heck out of Audrey, and she would not be able to resist his many charms. She was the sexiest woman he had ever met, and he had met quite a few. He also was drawn to her innocence, and how she seemed flustered whenever they were together. Her Achilles heel was ice cream, but a whipped cream toe-gasm had once sent her into ecstasy, and he would love to repeat it. But then, she had remembered Griff, her confounded wedding vows, and returned to reading some confounded book. Confound it, anyway.

Audrey had vowed *I do* to Griff long ago, had never strayed, until Logan. The Logan factor puzzled her because her brain said one thing and her heart another, and she didn't know what to do about either. Her heart shouted Logan and her brain whispered Griff.

Logan, couldn't get enough of Audrey. She set him afire, stirring him as no other woman had, and he craved more time with her. His infatuation with her reminded him of his high school years, fifteen years old, pimply-faced, and watching the cheerleaders swing their hips. Audrey didn't do any hip swinging; she didn't have to, because her mere presence set him aglow. He knew immediately that he would have walked the plank for her. He and Audrey had heated up, ready to do business several times, and Logan was persistent, but something always interrupted his moves, leaving him frustrated. She indicated she was interested, even more than interested, but her vows blocked her willingness to dive into a temporary or permanent relationship.

Audrey had played hard-to-get, which was fair because, after all, she had been married to the beast for nearly five decades. Her sons lived in

Oregon, and he didn't know about them. If they were like Griff, they could also be beasts and might come after him. On the one foot, he wasn't a home wrecker, but on the other, he refused to lose the one woman who had set his manliness ablaze. By whatever means, or apparently by no means, she had ignited his male organs to begin working again.

Now they had come to her town, Hunter. She was with Griff at her home and he was at the Hunter Inn, feeling abandoned and agonizing over his decision to have come, wondering if his quest was viable or not. The question arose: stay the course or throw in the towel? Easy answer: Stay the course. He hoped it wouldn't be long.

CHAPTER 10
Steve

Steve, a retired dentist, had married Carlee twenty years earlier as his trophy wife when she was forty and he fifty-eight. She loved sex and with a slim and trim physique, she was appealing and interesting. Through the years, he had aged well, growing more handsome, but she was the opposite, acquiring leathery wrinkles making her appear older than her years. His hair had changed from wavy black to a sexy salt and pepper while her black hair remained black, thanks to a talented cosmetologist. She wore it short in what her stylist called funky, hoping people would notice her hair, not her wrinkled skin. She recently had taken to wearing a silk scarf around her neck in an effort to conceal her turkey waddle.

Steve began losing his hearing during the first years of their marriage, and she had convinced him to purchase hearing aids, which helped, but weren't perfect. He forgot them, occasionally misplaced them, or turned the sound down, rendering them useless. It had been a never-ending battle. At his office, he removed the aids when he used his drill because the noise of the drill intensified the sound coming into his ears, forgetting to return them to his ears when he finished the procedure, and then sometimes leaving them at work when he called it a day.

The hearing aid batteries caused another problem. Steve had large hands. He had found a way to master the tiny dental tools but replacing batteries in the hearing aids was another problem. He could barely get them out of the package much less into his hearing aids. Carlee had grown weary of helping him, so at times his hearing aids stood battery-less and did not help at all, even serving as barriers for sound entering his ears.

The cruise had been a disaster after he had left his hearing aids in their hotel room prior to boarding the ship, and he spent two weeks unable to hear anything. Now, home a week, they still had not yet arrived. After twenty years of marriage, Carlee had learned to repeat conversations to make him understand what was being said, but her repetitions didn't always work either.

"Steve, why don't you buy a new set of hearing aids," Carlee suggested. "The old ones are four years old, and it's time for a new set anyway. You bought your last pair at Costco, so why don't you splurge and buy your next ones from one of the premium stores? We can write them off on our taxes, so they will cost less than they seem." Carlee was tired of repeating and translating what Steve didn't hear. After the two weeks at sea and one at home without any hearing aids, Carlee's tolerance shrank from slightly annoyed to full-bore irritated.

Steve didn't hear Carlee's suggestion, but responded, drawing out his words, "You know, Carlee, I've been thinking, I want to buy new hearing aids and not wait for the hotel in Fort Lauderdale to return the old ones. I don't think the hotel will send them. The old ones are four years old, the technology might have improved, and we can write them off on our taxes, meaning they'll cost less. And our insurance will pay something, too. I'll check with Costco to see if they upgraded their inventory. Their aids are cheaper than at the premium stores, but I'll look at the premium stores also. Don't argue with me about this because I want new ones. I wonder where Gus purchased his hearing aids. I'll call him. Or better yet, I'll go over to their house and see how they are. I would enjoy seeing Phyllis and Gus again." *Especially Phyllis.*

Steve had been attracted to Phyllis from the first time they met at the Air Force reunion, and she obviously enjoyed him. They managed to create time together on the cruise, and he wanted to take up where they left off. She carried a few extra pounds but was the sexiest woman he had ever met, including his wife Carlee. She smiled constantly, and her wild and curly ash-colored hair bounced as she spoke creating a whirling dervish image. She oozed charisma, and her sense of humor rocked off the charts. She laughed and teased while they did the horizontal hula, as she called it. Or the polka or the tango, she liked to say, any kind of bedsheet dancing. Steve thought that Gus was one lucky guy. Carlee was sexy and enthusiastic about sex, no doubt about it, offering herself to him as often as he was interested, but she was intense and consuming, while Phyllis had the perfect combination of playful humor and natural sexiness, and his libido spiked at her touch.

Carlee rolled her eyes. "Great idea, Steve, you get what you pay for. Maybe Costco carries high-end aids, as well as the less expensive ones, but buy the best you can find," Carlee added.

"I'll go to Costco this morning and check it out. Do we need anything?" Steve said, picking up his flat cap and heading out the door to the garage.

Steve didn't know how he would isolate Phyllis to enjoy her sexual charms, but he knew she would be willing, and perhaps she would have an idea. Their cruise ship lovemaking sessions had been simple. But now, back in Hunter, going around Gus, especially with his ill health, might prove difficult, although sex with Phyllis was worth the effort. He beamed as he thought about how sensual she was, muumuu and all.

CHAPTER 11
Phyllis

D r. Lewis stormed through the back door like a tsunami and asked, "How's my favorite patient doing today?"

Phyllis greeted, "He's better and I can't thank you enough, Dr. Lewis, for coming to see Gus. I tried to take him to our family doctor today, but he wants you, and no one else. He likes you, and you have been a lifesaver to nurse, or should I say doctor, Gus back to health. He walked up the stairs twice today without stopping and felt good. He says he is stronger and has been asking about you all afternoon. He's wondering why you aren't staying with us instead of the Hunter Inn."

"Stay here? Wouldn't that be an imposition? I wouldn't want to bother you, but it would make my life a little more pleasurable until I find my own apartment. Two flights? That's amazing, such a good sign," Dr. Lewis exclaimed.

Phyllis offered, "Sure, you are welcome to stay with us, we have two extra bedrooms, they are both on the second floor, and you can have either. I am proud of him, too, he seems to be making a real effort at losing some of his belly fat. He's moving more and eating less, and he's gonna trigger my guilt about my own love handles."

Because of inactivity and cruise menus, Gus and Phyllis struggled with their weight after leaving their full-time jobs. Watching their weight had been easy when they were busy all day, but without a strict schedule, they snacked and munched without regard. As the pounds went on, their once-active libido turned off, now downshifting from slow to nonexistent. Phyllis was alerted to her weight gain when the store clerks began showing her the muumuu racks, but Gus claimed to love her extra pounds, so she never bothered about diets. Her doctor didn't complain about her weight either, but Gus' doctor had advised him to address his weight issue. A panic attack sent him to the ship's medical center where Dr. Lewis laid down the law.

Phyllis picked up her keys and moved toward the door, "I need to go shopping, Dr. Lewis. As you know, I lost my charm bracelet and want to see if the jeweler can order another. I record my trip events with charms, but I guess the clasp snapped when it became too heavy, and I lost it. I hope I can buy one that has a better clasp. I'll be back in a while. Gus is lying down, resting from his stair-climbs."

"No problem, Phyllis, take your time. We have to calibrate and check his vitals, anyway." She moved to the bedroom where Gus was resting and closed the door, "Gus, Honey, how's my favorite patient doing today? Phyllis mentioned you made it up two flights of stairs today, and that's fantastic. Shall we have a trial run to see how your recovery is progressing? I can calibrate you, followed by my special cardio test."

Gus' clothes hit the floor in a flash, and Dr. Lewis' did the same. Thirty seconds later, they lay naked on the bed, stroking and caressing each other as if no time had passed since their last tryst three days before. They kissed and cuddled, and soon she was on top of him with a slow in-out, in-out before they fell apart, panting. A bead of sweat rolled down Gus' forehead into his eye. They lay in each other's arms for a few minutes until they heard the garage door open, and Gus hissed, "Oh, cripes! It's Phyllis!"

Phyllis was home earlier than she anticipated but paused to water her petunias and gather the mail from the mailbox before she entered the house. She called out, "Look, Gus, the jeweler had a similar bracelet in stock, so I bought five new charms, an airplane, a foot, a tooth, a beer bottle, and the number three to go with it. Aren't they pretty? I am finally ready for our next adventure! Where's Dr. Lewis?"

"Five charms are a lot. You should have bought a ship charm, but you can buy that later." Gus commented innocently as Dr. Lewis sneaked through the back door toward her car. "She just left, but she'll be back. She said you had invited her to stay with us, so she went to the hotel to gather her things. She should be back in a few minutes. It's a dandy idea to have her stay here. She offered to pay rent, but I told her that it is not necessary because we'd enjoy her being here, and we can spend more time with her calibration system, hopefully helping me to get better even sooner."

CHAPTER 12
Logan

Audrey was frustrated and angry at herself. She was married, and Logan was trying to steal her from Griff, and she wasn't resisting his advances as forcibly as she should. Logan insisted he wasn't a homewrecker, but when he had told her she was his soul and his very being, she had barely resisted being converted into an adulteress, and she wondered if a mental breakdown loomed in the near future. She was weary of Logan's relentless pursuit of her, but she didn't see him taking no for an answer. She liked him, in truth, she liked him a lot, maybe loved him, she didn't know for sure. Griff, with all his injuries and new retirement quirks, demanded an increasing amount of attention, and even before he had been hurt, he had become totally dependent on her. She loved Griff, had loved him forever, but now, she wasn't so sure. He had changed so much in recent years and hardly resembled the man she had married. And Logan didn't help. If only he would pack his bags and return to Portland, her life would return to normal. But would he leave? The only way to find out was to ask.

Audrey's reluctance to his advances was a new experience for Logan because women naturally swarmed to him like a magnet, including Joan before they married. His difficulty had been swishing them away, not attracting them. He knew that Audrey was interested, perhaps not interested enough to make her leave Griff right now, but he was a patient man. He had nothing currently urgent on his agenda and could bide his time until she came to her senses. Logan adored Audrey, and even though he had revealed his love, he wondered if she knew the extent of it. He was crazy for her, but she seemed ambivalent to his advances. Could he ever convince her to leave Griff behind?

They walked toward Logan's hotel when Audrey unexpectedly stopped, sat down on a park bench, and pulled him down beside her. She hadn't eaten breakfast and was famished, but this had to come first, "Logan, we need to talk, I'm having second thoughts about all of this."

Logan's eyes widened, and he frowned, saying, "Second thoughts? About me or Griff?" He noticed that her usually bright eyes looked tired.

"Well, both," she said. "When Dr. Lewis suggested that you and I have some alone time, I realized that's all we can ever have. Alone time, minutes or an hour now and then, brief encounters, stolen minutes, and the rest of the time…well, who knows? Relationships are not about stolen minutes, they are about continuous time together, dedicating ourselves to each other. I don't want stolen minutes, and I can't envision more time together in our future. I need time to hold your hand, kiss you, argue with you, and let you shower me with the attention I deserve and crave. We aren't getting younger, you're seventy, and I'm close behind, and as our time on this Earth dwindles down, you should return to Portland and forget about me and our stolen minutes' project, and I'll take Griff home and take care of him. It's my job. We are making a mistake, which will hurt Griff and our kids, yours and mine."

Logan replied, "Yes, stolen minutes, like right now, we're stealing time, and I'm the happiest that I have been in years because I love our stolen minutes, and you do, too. I don't want to leave Hunter until you have had enough time to sort through your out-of-control life, come to your senses, and be with me. I am willing to tolerate stolen minutes a little longer if that's the best we can do."

"But stolen minutes are just that, stolen, not really ours," Audrey countered. As she looked at Logan, her tired eyes pierced through him, and he knew she was serious.

"I have hope for us, Audrey, and I realize that you aren't ready to leave Griff right now, and sadly for me, I don't know if you ever will be. If you can never leave, so be it, and I'll have to be satisfied with our stolen minutes, but I'm not ready to ignore my emotions and the chance to have a life together. And one thing more, you should remember that you are Griff's wife, not his caretaker," Logan stated.

"But we take care of each other, that's part of being married all these years," Audrey countered.

Logan ignored her comments and continued, "I have never been happier and more certain of anything, and I am willing to bide my time until you are ready to leap off the loneliness bridge and leave Griff. Are you happy, Audrey?"

"That's a difficult question because yes, I am, and no, I'm not. I don't like complicated situations, but I'm drowning in complications, and I don't see a way out, other than breaking away from you. Breaking away from Griff means all kinds of sticky issues, from my kids to your kids, Griff, legal, financial. It's too complex. Breaking away from you means fewer complications, but…"

Logan interrupted and finished my sentence, "But, you will be happy. Happiness is important, especially at our ages, and you have the right to happiness. Who will make you happier, Audrey, Griff or me?"

CHAPTER 13
Audrey

"I can't force you to leave Hunter, Logan, and you are right. I need time to think about us, and me, and Griff, but at this minute I'm hungry, and I never make decisions on an empty stomach. I missed breakfast this morning, and now, I need to eat," Audrey pleaded, her growling stomach reminding her of her hunger. She realized that Logan was not really listening to what she was saying and would not go away easily.

She wanted the complications to go away, but life without Logan would mean she would return to her dreary, monotonous life. Her mind flashed to her long, lonely walks through the fields, listening to books, going days or sometimes weeks without seeing anyone except Griff. In good weather, she might initiate a lunch with Phyllis or Carlee or another friend, followed by a trip to the library to gather more books to read in silence. In the long winters, though, the silence captured her and became her world. The cruise had reminded her how little interaction she had with people other than Griff. She still loved Griff but had known for a long time that she needed more than him to be happy.

Audrey was fatigued, weary with Griff and his issues, but her conversation with Logan had tired her more. Why did everything have to be so complicated? Griff had become a demanding person after they married, and even more so with retirement, and now Logan was pressuring her to spend more time with him. She didn't know the answer to Logan's question. She loved them both, but differently.

Logan kissed her gently and recognized the fatigue, as her eyes had become bloodshot from tears or stress or both and hoped that his upcoming surprise would energize her. *Timing is everything*, he thought. *I hope this is the right time.* "Good idea. Let's go to the Hunter Inn and find something to eat," he offered with a smile, "my treat. They have a brunch with all kinds of items that cater to the yuppie crowd or whatever today's term is. They offer interesting dishes, like pizza with cauliflower and rutabaga crusts. The food mostly tastes good but different from the comfort food and greasy hamburgers and hot dogs you and I grew up eating. In fact, I ate seaweed yesterday, little leaflets of dried seaweed, but it tasted like alfalfa. I ate it, not all of it, but enough to know I didn't want to be a cow. It was disgusting, to say the least. Give me mac and cheese or a cheeseburger any day."

Audrey coughed out a laugh, "Seaweed? Really? It sounds awful. No, I have not eaten at the hotel. I tried to convince Griff to go, but he didn't want to. Too yuppie, he said. Do they have cheeseburgers? That would hit the spot." She was talking fast and jumping all over the place. Logan saw things logically, but she didn't.

"They have a good variety of eats. I had a hamburger the other day, and it was tasty, and I'd recommend it. And they have ice cream sundaes with real whipped cream," Logan winked at her and retrieved her hand. Logan, who had a self-proclaimed foot fetish, was recalling the dollops of whipped cream he had once spooned on Audrey's toes.

Audrey forced a smile and said, "A hamburger sounds wonderful, but I'm too tired for your version of a sundae. If Griff wakes up, someone will call me, but if he doesn't wake up soon, well, that's okay, too, because I could use a nap or at least rest my eyes. And my stomach is pleading for food."

"Let's go to my room before we eat," Logan said.

"That could be dangerous," Audrey scolded, but delighted in the idea of being alone with him. She had just told him to get lost, and now she was going to his room, and her lower forty was churning with something other than hunger pangs. She brushed something invisible from her arm as though trying to brush away her complications.

Logan pulled her toward the elevator where he punched four on the control panel. Audrey moaned, "We should have gone directly to the restaurant because I'm on the verge of fading away."

Logan whispered back, "Is your stomach all you're thinking about? Not about me? I'm crushed because I've been pining for you, for some stolen minutes, for some Audrey time."

"You've crossed my mind a time or two. I haven't left our house except to walk to the mailbox for the mail because Griff has consumed my time with his injuries, and now the broken foot. And perhaps a head injury."

"He has a clean break, and it'll heal quickly. Patience, Grasshopper."

"I'm famished, so can we at least order room service?" Audrey begged.

Logan slid his card across the key panel, and the door opened. A tea cart sitting in the center of the room held covered dishes of something. A bottle of uncorked wine, a dozen roses, and a box of chocolates sat perched on the desk.

Audrey's eyes brightened with pleasure, feeling immediately refreshed and squealed, "Oh, Logan, is this for us? What's under the plate cover?" She lifted the cover and found chicken parmesan with a large salad and French bread. "This is one of my faves. Thank you."

"Wait a minute, I have one more thing, actually two. Voila!" He pulled a carton of ice cream and a can of whipped cream from the mini fridge, held them up for her to see and placed them on the tea cart, "That's one."

"What a wonderful surprise. What's number two?" she asked, looking around, wondering what else he could attempt to lure her with.

Logan didn't say anything for a minute, and Audrey said, "Well? Where's number two? I'm starving."

Logan grinned sheepishly, not saying anything at first, but then, "I thought it would be so easy, and now I'm tongue-tied, but here it is. Number two coming right up: I love you, Audrey, and want to be with you now and always." He gathered her into his arms and kissed her.

CHAPTER 14
Audrey

Logan had dumbfounded Audrey with his unexpected declaration of love. Here she was, married to Griff for such a long time, yet, listening to someone she hardly knew announcing his love for her. It was unbelievable, yet she enjoyed hearing it and maybe on one level hoped it was true. Griff often said *I love you*, but he voiced it in a sort of passionless monotone and was usually followed by his suggestion to *do the dirty*. It grated on her like a scratchy record player. Logan's announcement had been filled with passion, and she felt it hotfoot through her body. His eyes had pierced through her like a magic arrow, and she had absorbed his kiss all the way to her toes, the way she smoldered when she and Griff first courted. Despite Griff's enthusiasm about sex, his kisses of late fizzled, leaving her lukewarm at best.

She returned to the hospital alone, walking slowly, mulling over what had transpired. Two hours ago, she had determined that Logan should return to Portland and leave her in Hunter to care for Griff. But he had different ideas and announced that he loved her, but what about Griff? More complications, which she didn't need right now.

Audrey's value system told her that marriage meant taking care of each other. She had cared for Griff through thick and thin, never complaining. He had cared for her, too, in his own way, but she wondered if he had lost the ability to see to her needs. Where did her obligation start or stop, or was there ever a stop?

"Oh, Audrey, you're here. I woke up a while ago and you were gone.

I didn't know where you went," Griff whined, scratching for her hand with his moist and limp paw. He looked pathetic with his black and blue nose and swollen eye where he had smashed his head on the floor. The swelling in his foot had gone down, but no cast yet. He answered her unasked question, "Tomorrow, maybe. I'm glad you're back to take care of me. Where did you go?"

"I was starving and went to eat. I had some chicken parmesan," she replied truthfully. Griff didn't need to know about the chocolate, flowers, and especially not about the ice cream and love declaration. She changed the subject. "Are you in pain? You have a doozy, of a shiner and your nose has puffed up like a fat chicken."

"Did you tell the boys about my fall? I don't want them to know because they'll think I'm frail. All this is Logan's fault, anyway, everything from the bunion to the broken foot. He did it," Griff growled. "But don't tell the boys."

"Logan didn't do anything except put the bunion splint on your toe because you had so much pain. You did the rest, so don't bring Logan into this," Audrey commented flatly.

"You're taking his side, and I don't like it," Griff complained.

Audrey didn't answer but was checking off her pros and cons as he spoke. Her mental list had grown longer. Pro: married forty-eight years. Con: married forty-eight years. Pro: Logan was a kind and gentle soul. Con: Griff used to be kind but had lapsed into a rather difficult person over the last several years. Pro: She had never strayed from Griff before the cruise. Con: She couldn't say she was faithful anymore but whose fault was that? She wasn't ready to take the blame, but maybe she should. Pro: Logan was romantic and stirred her sexually. Con: Griff wanted nothing to do with romance but wanted to continue his three-a-days. Pro: When Logan looked at her, she felt joy. Con: When Griff looked at her, she felt tired.

She offered Griff water and some pureed fruit while she continued making her mental list.

What did Griff want? Three-a-days. Someone to take care of him. A cook and a maid. TV. Fishing. Hunting. Travel, possibly. He wasn't overly warm to his grandkids, but he enjoyed them.

What did Logan want? Romance. Sex. Her. She didn't know about the cooking and cleaning business, but he had a housekeeper so maybe not. Conversation. Activity. Travel, probably. He didn't have grandchildren, and she didn't know how he would react to hers.

What did she want? Romance. Sex, but not three times a day. Conversation. Company. Humor. Activity. Travel, for sure. Opportunity to see her kids and grandkids more often. Logan would offer all of them. Griff could offer two or three, on a good day.

The list was growing, and her brain was muddling up, so she temporarily abandoned her list-making exercise and said, "Well, Griff, what's our next adventure." Perhaps his answer would help her sort out her emotions and give her direction.

Griff looked at her, and his eyes told her that he loved her, "I gotta get well before we do anything, but I'm thinking maybe we could try a trip to France. You've always wanted to go and can speak French. I don't like French food much, but I'm willing to give it a go. We could take a cruise or just fly to France, whichever you want. It would be fun. I've heard that the French like sex and I'm all in on that. Maybe the rest of the gang would go, too, you know, a repeat trip. Not Logan, though. I don't want to ever see that quack again."

"I didn't expect you to say a trip to France. And the French are known for romance, not sex, Griff," Audrey murmured, still wondering about Griff versus Logan.

CHAPTER 15
Phyllis

Two days later, Dr. Lewis came by with her SUV, two suitcases, a large bag of food, and a six-pack of red and white wines. She brought them into the house and set them near the front door. She said, "Thanks so much for having me! I don't have too much by way of belongings because I mostly used the ship's uniforms. One of these days I need to go shopping. It's a lucky thing the hospital provides me with scrubs, or I'd be a naked baby."

"Hunter doesn't have much shopping, so you might want to head to Boise or Salt Lake. Even Pocatello is better than Hunter. I could go with you if you'd like," Phyllis said.

"I was thinking Denver, which has several large malls, and I could shop my heart out. I want Gus to go so that I can see how the calibration system is working in real life," Dr. Lewis explained. "It would be an overnight trip, maybe two."

"Denver? That's a day away. Pocatello is an hour or so and Salt Lake City is not more than three. I don't think Gus is well enough to go that far." Phyllis didn't like her idea, even though she was his doctor.

"I would be with him and would take care of him. That's what we doctors do," Dr. Lewis replied coolly.

Phyllis' mind was racing. Sure, Dr. Lewis had taken care of Gus and sure, he was better, and sure, Phyllis liked her, but she seemed a little too eager to tend to her husband, her Gus, and she didn't like the idea of Gus going off with anyone, not even Dr. Lewis. She wanted to know what this calibration system entailed and how it worked.

"Dr. Lewis, could you explain the calibration system to me in plain words? I don't know what it is or how it works, and I don't understand *doctor talk*. I could help Gus if I understood it better," Phyllis said, trying to put a good light on a nebulous situation.

She didn't answer the question, but said, "Oh, sure, we can get to that. In the meantime, I bought a few groceries and wine, too, although Gus shouldn't be drinking wine. I want to pay my fair share, and Gus insisted that he didn't want me to pay rent. You and I can enjoy some wine, I brought plenty of both red and white."

Gus came out of their bedroom, "You came, Dr. Lewis, good, we're glad to see you." Gus had brightened up with rosy cheeks, sparkling eyes, and he was no longer shuffling, rather bounced as he walked. He wore his purple bathrobe with his Hunter High School baseball cap perched atop his head.

"How long are you planning to stay in Hunter, Dr. Lewis?" Phyllis asked.

Dr. Lewis tended not to answer questions but went off in her own direction. "My calibration system is working. Just look at Gus! He looks great, better than I've ever seen him; he's truly on the mend. I'd like to increase calibration to more than once a day. Maybe that would speed up his recovery even more. I could sleep downstairs and would be able to check on Gus multiple times in the night, and if he needed extra calibration, I could give it to him right then, right there. Could you set up an extra bed in your bedroom? I'll calibrate twice a day, morning and evenings and that should do the trick for his heart issues. I wouldn't want to wake you, Phyllis, so could you sleep upstairs in one of your guest rooms? It would be in Gus' best interest."

Phyllis was appalled by Dr. Lewis' request to sleep with Gus and move her upstairs. The whole calibration system had her in a dither, and she regretted inviting her to stay. She didn't want Dr. Lewis to take Gus to Denver or even Pocatello, in fact, she didn't want to be away from him at all. Yet, Gus was better, rosy cheeks and reduced shuffling. But Phyllis was not.

Phyllis repeated her question for the third time, "What is calibration anyway? Can you explain it? I mean Gus might understand it, but I don't, and I'm curious. Are we going to have to submit this to our health insurance company? I need to know because we might need to obtain pre-authorization."

"No, you don't have to apply with your insurance company," Dr. Lewis said, finally answering one of Phyllis' questions. She added quickly, "It's a new system, and it isn't yet covered by insurance, but don't worry, I'm not going to bill you. I'm doing it because I love Gus," she paused, "and you, of course." Dr. Lewis picked up her suitcases and aimed herself at Gus and Phyllis' first floor bedroom. "I'll put the groceries away in a jif, and I've got more bags of groceries in the car."

That was a relief because paperwork for insurance was a nightmare, and Phyllis knew that hospital and medical bills can add up quickly if they were experimental and not approved. Phyllis still wanted to know what the calibration system was, but at this point, she doubted Dr. Lewis would answer.

Gus stood up abruptly, grabbed his chest, and collapsed to the couch, then slid to the floor. "Oh, God, I'm hurting, Phyllis, Dr. Lewis, somebody, call 911. It feels like I have an elephant jumping on my chest and I might be having another panic attack or worse, a heart attack."

CHAPTER 16
Phyllis

Phyllis called 911 and requested an ambulance for Gus and shouted for Dr. Lewis who was toting another bag of something into the house. Dr. Lewis heard the shout and dashed into the house and assessed his condition. "Gus, Honey, you aren't having a panic attack, you are having a full-blown heart attack. Breathe easy, the EMTs will fix you up and take you to the hospital. They should arrive in a jiffy. Phyllis, grab whatever pills he takes and bring them with you. You can drive your car, and I'll accompany Gus in the ambulance. Tell me where you hurt, Gus, Honey."

He pointed to his chest, his arm, and clasped his shoulder. "Everywhere. It's moving around, but mostly my chest," he panted. "Fix it, Phyllis." His strained words were barely decipherable and *fix it* sounded like *fisst*. His face and neck colored red, and his eyes closed and opened and closed and opened, more glazed than focused.

Dr. Lewis raced back to her car and returned with a stethoscope urging, "Stay steady, Gus, I'm here."

Phyllis didn't want to leave Gus' side, and held his hand, holding it to her chest. "Oh, my darling Gus, hang on."

The EMTs arrived, attached Gus to machines, and loaded him into the ambulance while Phyllis retrieved his pills, her keys, and her purse. She backed her Chevy Cruze out of the driveway and aimed it at the Hunter Hospital, only a mile away. The ambulance was rounding the first corner as she sped down the street. The siren released the first and second stop lights and the ambulance sped through, but Phyllis caught both lights and lost sight of them.

The lead EMT instructed the driver, "Pocatello General, we need to take him to Poky, even though it's several miles farther. Hunter doesn't have what Mr. Gustafson needs."

Dr. Lewis clutched Gus' hand and massaged his face, and he rolled his eyes once and closed them, squeezed Dr. Lewis hand, and gasped, "Solly, Phylss, so solly love you. Don't love her, love you, Phylss. Solly." The machines continued to tremble and jump, and tears poured down Dr. Lewis' cheeks.

They were over halfway to Pocatello when the ambulance driver said, "Pocatello General radioed me, they are full. We've gotta take him back to Hunter, so hang on." With no wide spot to make a U-turn, he executed a proper three-point turn and headed back to Hunter.

CHAPTER 17
Phyllis

Phyllis arrived at Hunter Hospital within minutes, but the ambulance was nowhere in sight. She handed her keys to the teenaged parking attendant and beelined herself to the emergency room to wait for Gus, Dr. Lewis, and the EMTs. The ER was bustling at that moment, and as she circled throughout the room, she poked her head into each of the curtained cubicles, causing gasps, glares, and scowls by patients and families in assorted stages of undress. The staff eyed her suspiciously and repeated *he's not here yet* over and over, but she kept searching. After a time, she exited the building and walked to the vacant ambulance entrance. No lights, no sirens, no ambulance. "Where are they?" She asked herself and returned to the nurses' station to repeat the question.

"As far as we know, no ambulances are headed this way. Are you sure the EMTs said Hunter Hospital?" Matt, the head nurse, asked. "Could they have taken him to Poky? The EMTs sometimes take heart attack cases to Pocatello General."

"Could you call them, please? I was in such a panic I left my cell phone at home," she asked.

"Sure, no problem," Matt agreed.

Phyllis continued to pace as Matt phoned Pocatello General. She ran her eyes over and around his buff body and shook off those thoughts.

Matt interrupted her thoughts by shaking his head, "No ambulances, no walk ins, no nothing, I'm sorry, Mrs. Gustafson." Phyllis was puzzled. *Where had the EMTs and Dr. Lewis taken Gus?*

49

Phyllis and Gus' house was located an easy ten minutes from the hospital, so she zipped home to get her phone, wondering what happened to the ambulance and if something worse happened. Without her cell phone, she didn't have Dr. Lewis' number and knew that Gus obviously wouldn't have his phone either.

The ambulance had disappeared and so had Gus and Dr. Lewis. *Had the EMTs kidnapped Gus? Or had Dr. Lewis kidnapped them all?* Between the calibration system and her seeming obsessions with Gus, Phyllis' imagination was starting to run amok. *Could they have been... you know... doing the horizontal hula or some other monkey business? No, no way. Gus was in the middle of a heart attack and she was a doctor. Hippocratic Oath and all that. Phyllis! Get a hold of yourself!*

Her phone jangled, and she looked at the screen. *Thank God. Dr. Lewis.*

"Where are you?" Phyllis greeted Dr. Lewis. "Did you have an accident? I waited for you in the ER, but you didn't come."

Dr. Lewis apologized, "I'm so sorry, Phyllis. So sorry. We started to Pocatello General because they have a better heart unit, but..."

Phyllis interrupted her, "But, what? Okay, Pocatello General. I'll drive to Pocatello and arrive in about an hour. Tell Gus I'm on my way." Phyllis clicked off before Dr. Lewis had a chance to finish her sentence.

CHAPTER 18
Phyllis

Phyllis had already left the conversation, and Dr. Lewis continued talking to an empty phone, "We are returning to Hunter. Don't leave, hang tight. I'm not sure where we are going." She heard the phone click off, but called out, "Phyllis? Phyllis. Don't go," It was too late, and Phyllis didn't hear her say anything as she backed her car out of the driveway.

Even though the sunlight was fading, she drove like a maniac. With few cars on the road, she overtook them all, dodging in and out of traffic when without warning her Cruze sputtered and groaned and two different dashboard lights flickered on. The red oil light and a flickering-yellow exclamation mark groaned that her beloved car had been taken for granted long enough. The car was less than a year old, so the warnings were unexpected. "Oh, frack," she swore, "what the…"

As she eased to the side of the highway, an ambulance sped by, pointed toward Hunter with lights and sirens blaring, definitely in a hurry.

She viewed the landscape. Sagebrush, dry hills, a coyote chasing a jackrabbit, but no lights or buildings, not even electric wires and the sky was growing dark. She sighed and pulled out her cell phone, but it had no bars. *Frack, frack, double frack.* She sat behind the wheel and considered what to do. Walk to Pocatello? No, she wasn't even halfway, and it would be night before she arrived. Should she flag someone down? God knows who would stop. Should she sit in her car and wait for law enforcement or someone she knew?

She turned on her emergency signal and got out of the car. The night air had a bite, and she pawed through the backseat for a jacket or sweater and found none, but instead found an old scarf. She wrapped it around herself, and although it offered little protection from the elements, it was better than nothing. Several cars whipped by, but in the wrong direction, and they apparently didn't notice her, a damsel in distress. She began waving the scarf at the passing vehicles, but still no one slowed down or noticed her standing on the side of the road. She felt invisible. Cold, frustrated, and on the verge of tears, she returned to the Cruze.

Finally, a van passed, slowed, stopped, and backed up. It was navy blue with a few dents and scratches, and the rear was covered with faded and torn bumper stickers. "Can we help you, lady?" a male voice from the van called through the passenger window. She couldn't see into the interior but made out the shapes of two or three people.

"I need to go to Pocatello, and I'm waiting for my husband," which wasn't much of a lie, but she hesitated to say she was alone.

"We can take you," the voice offered, as three men exited the van. They were all in their thirties with heavy unkempt beards, wearing denim pants, plaid shirts, and cowboy hats. Under different circumstances, she might have considered all three of them good-looking, maybe a charm bracelet possibility, but right here and right now in the fading sunlight, they frightened her. All three stood before her, and she didn't know how to stop them.

The person who had been riding in the suicide seat said, "We work at a ranch five miles east and are going to Pocatello for dinner and to whoop it up a bit, but we haven't started whooping yet. We won't harm you, lady, we'd like to help you. You'll be lucky to see two or three cars in the next hour. It's supper time."

The man who had been in the back of the van used a flashlight to light up her face, making it impossible for her to see him before he said, "Mrs. Gustafson! I'm Danny Main, one of your former students. Don't you remember me? I was the one who stole your stapler and tape from your desk every day. I had quite a stash when I graduated. We'll take you to Pocatello, don't worry about a thing," he chuckled as he moved toward her. "It's good to see you."

CHAPTER 19
Phyllis

The three bearded young men dropped her at Pocatello General where she knew Gus would be. She entered the ER and looked around but didn't see either Dr. Lewis or Gus. She asked the receptionist what his room number was, but they had no record of him either. She swiped open her cell phone, intending to call Dr. Lewis, with the questions *Where are you, and what the heck did you do with Gus* in the forefront of her mind, but her phone's battery symbol had turned bright red, meaning not only no bars, but also no battery power. What else can go wrong? She didn't know Dr. Lewis' number and was at a loss as to what to do, but thought about alternative ways of returning to Hunter, where could she find help. Griff? He was using a wheelchair. Audrey? Maybe, but she was tied up with Griff. Carlee? Probably not. Steve? That's who: Steve. He would come to her rescue. She knew he would help her, but didn't know his phone number, however, Audrey's number was locked in her brain, and she asked to use the emergency room desk phone.

"Audrey, this is Phyllis. I'm in trouble and I need help."

Audrey listened carefully, "Phyllis, what's wrong, what do you need?"

"Gus had a heart attack today, and the EMTs transported him to Pocatello, except he never arrived. Now I'm at the Pocatello hospital and he hasn't been seen and he's not at the Hunter Hospital either and also, my new Cruze broke down while I was driving to Pokey and is parked on the side of the road, a few miles out, and I have to find Gus, and I need someone to take my car back to Hunter. And I need an anti-stress pill, but don't have one." Her sentences ran together, and her voice quivered. Maybe she could convince one of the nurses to loan her an anti-stress pill.

Audrey said, "Whoa! Calm down, Phyllis. Gus had a heart attack? Oh, no! Is he okay?"

"Probably, but I don't know for sure. Dr. Lewis went with him to the Pocatello hospital, but they never arrived. You are busy with Griff, but could you call Steve and ask him to pick me up? I don't know who else to ask," Phyllis was in tears and sobbed out the last sentence.

"I'm with Griff right now," Audrey said, "but I'll figure out something. I'll call Steve, so call me back in five minutes and I'll tell you who's coming to drive you back to Hunter. If Steve can't come, maybe Logan can drive to Pocatello," Audrey said. "I'll call him, too."

"Great, you're a lifesaver, thanks, Audrey."

Audrey dialed Steve's number, letting it ring several times, but he didn't answer. She waited a couple more minutes before she redialed. Steve didn't hear it ring but felt the phone buzzing and started talking. "Carlee? Is that you? You sound different. Is something wrong with the phone? I'm at Costco looking at hearing aids. Do we need anything while I'm here?"

Audrey shouted into the phone and slowed her speech pattern, "Steve, listen to me, this is Audrey, not Carlee. Audrey, Griff's wife. Gus had a heart attack, but Phyllis is stranded without a car in Pocatello and needs to come back to Hunter. She wants you to drive to Pocatello to pick her up."

Despite her increased volume, Steve heard little, and decided to remove himself from the conversation, "That's fine, Carlee, I'll be home soon, because I'm almost finished at Costco. We can drive to Pocatello for dinner if you'd like. That would be fine." With that he closed his flip phone.

Audrey punched the off button on her phone and went into the hall to dial Logan, who knew nothing of Gus' medical condition, but she dispensed with a greeting or niceties. "Can you drive to Pocatello to bring Phyllis back? Steve thought I was Carlee and didn't hear anything I was trying to say, so I gave up. The bottom line is that somebody has to drive to Pocatello for Phyllis. With Griff in the hospital, I can't leave, so would you mind picking her up and bringing her back to Hunter?"

"Oh, sure, but I'd rather spend time with you and your hot-flash riddled body, but for you, I'll retrieve Phyllis. Tell me again, why am I doing it? How far is Pocatello?" Logan answered. "Do you think Phyllis will mind if I come instead of Steve?"

Audrey smiled and said, "Gus had a heart attack, and she's stranded but Pocatello isn't that far. By the way, I loved the surprises today, the flowers and chocolate and…I'm much better. Thank you."

"Is that all you liked?" Logan persisted, "what about the other things."

"We haven't eaten the ice cream, but we can sample it later," Audrey resisted half-laughing because she knew he wasn't talking about ice cream.

Logan frowned, "And what about my profession of love for you? Did you like that, or was I too bold?"

"I did like it, and it was bold, scary, and charming, all at the same time," Audrey said.

"Scary? Charming? Are those your responses?" Logan pouted.

"No, I need time to process your words, and sort out what to say to you, but right now you have to rescue Phyllis and I have to check on Griff."

CHAPTER 20
Phyllis

An hour later, Logan helped Phyllis into his Mercedes rental, and she asked, "Have you heard anything about Gus or seen Dr. Lewis? She rode with Gus in the ambulance to take him to the Pocatello hospital, but they never arrived, and no one knows where they are. And two emergency signals came on my Cruze, and I parked it on the side of the road halfway between Hunter and Pocatello. Everything's going wrong, and I'm beside myself. Do you think they moved him to another hospital, maybe Salt Lake or Boise? My phone is dead, so I haven't received any calls." Her voice cracked as she spoke, and Logan feared she would start crying.

Phyllis' mind focused on Gus, and she was weak with worry and needed solace until she could be with her darling husband again. Dealing with hard times was difficult for Phyllis, and today was the worst. She needed support from whomever was available, and today Logan was available. She knew Logan was crazy for Audrey, but he was a doctor and comforting people was in their DNA. She hoped he didn't mind.

She skimmed her eyes over him and breathed deeply. Dabbing her teary eyes with a tissue, she moved her left hand to Logan's right knee, pulling herself closer. "You don't mind, do you, Logan? I need to be close to someone now. Gus is my whole shebang and I am afraid of losing him."

Logan glanced at her hand resting on his knee and peeked at her, as if deciding what to do. She had come on to him previously, but he was wild for Audrey, and obviously had to discourage Phyllis especially when he knew that Gus could be dying or even dead by now. Heart attacks could go either way. Phyllis was obviously distraught, and he was a doctor but it was not his responsibility to provide this kind of support.

He turned his head to stare at her feet, and she wondered what he was thinking. Who was it that mentioned he had a foot fetish? Audrey? Carlee? She wore loafers with no toes showing so his foot fetish might be a no-go. Dang. She had never been with someone who had a foot fetish. He might or might not mind her hand on his knee, and she thought about moving it, but instead, she stretched her hand farther up his thigh.

Logan looked at her hand a time or two. She could see the wheels turning, *does she or doesn't she mean anything by placing her hand on his leg,* but he didn't say anything and left her hand where it was. He must have figured out what she was thinking, and a moment later he reached over to pat her leg, "It'll be fine, Phyllis. Gus will pull through. Don't worry, we'll find him."

Even though Gus consumed Phyllis' mind, he wasn't in the car, so she decided to push the envelope and allowed her hand to creep toward his crotch to see what he would do.

He jumped at her touch and jerked the steering wheel to the right. He hit gravel, and slid down the embankment. The car didn't roll, but airbags ejected, she shrieked, and the Mercedes fishtailed to a stop.

The airbags deflated immediately, and they sat for a minute before they started to stir. Logan croaked out as if he had a frog in his throat, "Are you all right?"

"Yes, I'm okay. I don't think anything's broken but my arm hurts a little. How about you?" she asked as she rubbed her right arm. "Your nose is bleeding." She rummaged through her purse for tissues.

Logan dabbed at his nose with a tissue, which came away red. He picked up a second tissue, spiraled it, and stuck it in his nostril. It also turned red. "Yes, I'm dripping, but the rest of me seems okay. It'll stop bleeding in a second. Can you open the door? My door is jammed so if you can push yours open, you can exit easily enough, and I'll crawl over to your side. Afterwards, I'll look at your arm."

"I'm pushing, but I'm not strong enough, and it's my right arm that hurts," she complained.

"I can crawl over you to push the door open. Can you move your seat back to give me more room?" Logan offered as he pulled himself up and straddled first the console, then Phyllis to push the passenger door open.

She couldn't believe it: Her heart skipped a beat and her upper body began to heat up. *Not now, don't get all rosy cheeked right now*, she scolded herself. *Logan? Maybe he isn't so tied up with Audrey after all. Maybe she had a chance. After all, she already had purchased the foot charm.*

They exited the car and stood on the side of the road, hoping someone would come by. Phyllis looked up and down the road. She had been stranded nearby a few hours earlier and knew her car was close. A light flashed high above the road, and she figured it was the cell tower where her car was parked. She pointed at it and exclaimed, "My car. It's parked on the side of the road near the cell tower, and I'm chilly. We can warm up inside it."

Logan used his state-of-the-art cell phone to dial 911 to request assistance. He wanted a tow truck and a ride to Hunter, nothing more, but he knew they would send an army of EMTs. He affirmed that her shoulder wasn't dislocated or broken, even though she had a little pain that streamed from between her shoulder and fingers.

They walked to her Cruze, and Phyllis said, "The back seat is more comfortable, and I can lie down and rest my shoulder. It hurts, and the EMTs won't arrive for a while. Can I use your lap for a pillow?"

She placed her head on Logan's lap and he began to stroke her hair straightening her tangles after the encounter with the airbags. She could feel him getting nervous. Under any other circumstances, she would no doubt have responded differently, instead she said, "Not now, Logan, you know, Gus…" His demonstration of nerves gave her a boost of confidence that she hadn't lost her touch.

CHAPTER 21
Phyllis

The emergency personnel, six in all, arrived in three vehicles, a firetruck, an ambulance, and a sheriff's four by four. All three vehicles had lights and sirens blaring for all to hear. A private tow truck followed close behind with two workers, but they found nobody in or around the Mercedes.

"Where the heck are they? Did someone pick them up?" one of the EMTs asked.

Logan and Phyllis extracted themselves from her car, and he called, "Here, we're here!"

They walked down the incline to the Mercedes, through a gauntlet formed by the emergency personnel. The EMTs opened the back of the ambulance and withdrew several pieces of equipment, and one began examining Logan and the other assessed Phyllis. A third and fourth opened iPads and began typing.

EMT: What's your name, Ma'am? Could I see your identification?

Phyllis: Phyllis Gustafson. My ID is in my purse, which is in the car, the other car.

EMT: You have two cars?

Phyllis: No, I have one. The Cruze. The Mercedes belongs to Logan.

EMT: Are you Logan? Logan what?

Logan: Yes, Logan Hall, I was driving the Mercedes, but it's a rental, and the paperwork is inside.

EMT: Who was driving?

Logan: I was driving.

Phyllis: Yes, Logan was driving and uh, something distracted him, and he swerved down the embankment.

EMT: Were you on your cell phone, Mr. Hall? Is that how you became distracted?

Logan and Phyllis: Not really. Nope.

EMT: What distracted you, Mr. Hall?

Logan: Dr. Hall. I'm a podiatrist.

EMT: Phyllis Gustafson. I saw you earlier today at your house, when your husband Gus had a heart attack, right? We went to Pocatello General but transported him back to Hunter.

Phyllis: I've been looking for him. Is he back in Hunter?

EMT: Yes, he's back in Hunter. But wait, you're not the same Mrs. Gustafson because she had black hair and a red sweater. You can't be Mrs. Gustafson because she was in the ambulance with us. Are there two Phyllis Gustafsons?

Phyllis: That would be Dr. Lewis. She's going to stay with Gus and me until she rents her own place. She's Gus' doctor.

EMT: No, I'm sure she said she was his wife. She was extremely upset about Gus.

Logan: Can you take us to Hunter? We need to find Gus.

EMT: Yes, Gus, well, let's go find him.

The firetruck departed, and the EMTs finished a cursory examination of the two, noting nothing serious, so the sheriff volunteered to transport Logan and Phyllis to Hunter. Except for Logan's bloody shirt from the nosebleed and Phyllis' sore shoulder, nothing else was damaged and at last they knew where Gus was.

CHAPTER 22
Phyllis

The sheriff left Logan and Phyllis at the Hunter emergency room entrance where they inquired about Gus. Phyllis had been in the ER a few hours earlier looking for Gus, and now she was repeating her previous questions. "Where is Gus?"

Logan said, "This is crazy. If he's not here or in Pocatello, where else could he be? Is he at home? Is he d...?"

She caught on. "Dead? Is he dead? He can't be because someone would have told me. Dr. Lewis would have told me, but my cell phone died. Oh, frack, both my car and my cell phone died. And maybe Gus. Where is he?" She was beside herself with the thought of her honey being dead. "No...he can't be."

Matt, the head nurse, buzzed around the ER and said, "I don't know, Mrs. Gustafson. I could call down to the morgue to see what I can find out."

"Morgue? My Gus. Oh, no, it can't be," she sobbed as a waterfall spilled from her eyes to her cheeks, taking her mascara with it. The entire emergency room, including staff, patients, and families, rotated their bodies to stare at her and Logan.

Logan put his arms around her and held her close. "Be calm, be calm," he cooed as Matt moved them to a private sitting room where she continued to weep. He held her while she cried, and she felt comforted. "Logan...you're..."

Matt returned to the private room and sat down next to Phyllis, "No, Mrs. Gustafson, I'm sorry, he's alive, and I spoke with his doctor, a Dr.

Lewis, who suggested checking for him at the Big Pine Hospital on the other side of town."

"We don't have cars," Logan said. "Your Cruze died, and I wrecked my Mercedes. The tow truck should have taken them to a garage. Audrey is upstairs with Griff, I think, but she doesn't have a car either because she rode with Griff in the ambulance."

They punched the elevator button to the third floor and found Griff's room. He had fallen asleep again, but Audrey was leafing through some old magazine. She brightened up when she saw them.

Phyllis was glad to see Audrey, too. Audrey hugged Phyllis and asked about Gus. She hugged Logan, too, but the hug was more of an embrace, longer than a quick hug, and he kissed her on the cheek, also a little longer than it needed to be, giving Phyllis enough time to think *GAR, get a room* before they separated.

This would give Phyllis something to ponder, and she perked up a bit suggesting, "Because we don't have our own vehicles, we can Uber it. You know, call an Uber. I have the app on my phone, but I haven't used it." She swore, "Oh frack, everything's dead, my car, my phone, but thankfully not Gus, so that's a good thing."

CHAPTER 23
Phyllis

Logan installed the Uber app on his phone, clicked a few clicks, and arranged a pickup in fifteen minutes. Griff rallied and wanted to go, too, but Audrey nixed that. The Uber driver was a skinny girl with pink hair and a pin-cushioned face filled with silver piercings that looked like paper clips. She was driving a mini car, maybe a Cooper, and introduced herself as Tequila as her eyes fell on Phyllis. They crammed themselves into the Uber, and Tequila asked, "The order says the hospital, but that's where we are now. Do you have an address?"

Phyllis answered, "Your name isn't Tequila, your name is Suzy. Suzy Rush. Your hair was different, maybe long and not pink, and you didn't have a face full of jewelry, but I remember you. You took my language arts class a few years ago, before I retired. You were a good student, why aren't you in college?"

Tequila responded, "Oh, Ms. Gustafson, I didn't recognize you, and I changed my name to Tequila. I drive Uber to pay for college. It works out well. How's Mr. Gustafson?"

Phyllis' eyes started leaking again, "I don't know. Mr. Gustafson...my Gus...he had a heart attack and now I can't find him, but we think he's at the other hospital."

"A heart attack? I'm so sorry. He was my gym teacher, and we all loved him. It's so sad," Tequila responded, gaping at Phyllis in the rear-view mirror.

"Can't you Google the address for the hospital?" Audrey asked. "Google knows everything."

"I did, but nothing came up. No address, just the name Big Pine, but it's on the other side of town so I only have a general idea where it is," Tequila replied. "I'll try again, and if he's not at Big Pine, you can call me to return you to the Hunter Hospital."

The sign on the front of the building read *Big Pine* and Tequila dropped them in the parking lot. She hugged Phyllis and handed her a card with her contact information. Phyllis and Audrey thought they knew the town well, but neither had ever seen this hospital before. It was small, a single-story building with only four cars in the parking lot. They looked at each other and shrugged.

The reception room was small, with an empty reception desk that held only a small bell that was marked with adhesive tape saying, *ring bell for service.* She rang several times before standing silent, waiting for service or a greeter or somebody who would acknowledge their presence. After a long minute or two, Phyllis jammed the bell several more times. Ding, ding, ding. Finally, a tall, sad-faced woman entered through a door behind the desk. She was dressed in a lab coat and her long unkempt hair wisped over her shoulders. She wore round, rimless eyeglasses with a pink hue. Logan noted that she was seeing life *through rose-colored glasses.* Her name badge read *Deanna, Deputy Coroner.*

"Wait," Phyllis cried, "is this the Big Pine Hospital? Is Gus here?"

"No, it's the Big Pine morgue," Deanna said. "We don't have a Gus here. The hospital is on the other side of town."

"Oh, frack," Phyllis exclaimed. "Frack, frack, frack. I'll never find Gus."

CHAPTER 24
Phyllis

Logan contacted Tequila who was able to get them back to the Hunter Hospital where they would try to locate Gus once more. Audrey also wanted to check on Griff, but they needed to find out the location of the Big Pine Hospital. The only Big Pine that appeared on GPS was a morgue, and Gus wasn't there, and neither Audrey, Phyllis, nor Tequila had any idea where the Big Pine Hospital was.

When they arrived at Hunter Hospital, Audrey hurried to the elevator, while Logan and Phyllis consulted the puzzled front desk and asked the receptionist the whereabouts of the Big Pine Hospital. "Hunter has a single hospital, this one but some of the staff call the morgue Big Pine Hospital as a joke, but it's no hospital. Anyone goin' in, ain't comin' out. Who are you looking for?" she quipped.

Phyllis recited Gus' name and the day's events, including her trip to the morgue, and she shook her head. "I don't know why, but someone was messing with your head because Mr. Gustafson is on the third floor. Take the elevator to floor three and turn left. It's on that hall. I am sure he'll be glad to see you."

Phyllis and Audrey followed the receptionist's instructions while Logan searched for coffee, and soon, they stood in the doorway of a room peeking in at Gus. And Griff. Two beds, two men, Gus and Griff both in the same room. Gus had been seen and moved from the ICU while they were looking for him and was currently sedated. A myriad of gadgets and gismos were hooked up to his torso, but Phyllis didn't know what any of them measured. Gus was sound asleep, and it was doubtful if he knew or cared about what they did. Dr. Lewis sat near the bed playing with her cell phone and looked up as they entered. She looked as if she had been crying and didn't connect eyes with Phyllis. "You found us. You wouldn't believe the adventure we had."

"Us, too," Phyllis said. "We have been all over and ended up at the morgue. You wouldn't believe it. They call it..."

Dr. Lewis interrupted Phyllis, "I know, they call it the Big Pine Hospital, but it's really the morgue. I'm sorry."

Phyllis picked up Gus' hand and kissed it, saying, "How is he? Did they do surgery, or what?"

As usual, Dr. Lewis didn't answer Phyllis' question, but said, "He'll be fine. He told me that he loves you. I expected the calibrations to help, but they didn't. And he loves you, not me."

Dr. Lewis had done everything she could think of to gain Gus' affection, to have him for her own. She had been sure she could win him over, but in the end, Gus had chosen Phyllis. She recalled his labored words in the ambulance, *Solly, Phylss, so solly love you. Don't love her, love you, Phylss. Solly.* It had been a painful blow to her ego, but she would have to face the reality. Gus loved Phyllis.

"Thank you, Dr. Lewis, thank you for everything, especially for staying with Gus while I chased a wild goose throughout Hunter looking for him," Phyllis said, "but, how is he?"

"Take care of Gus, he's my special one, the most special one," Dr. Lewis sputtered, obviously choked up. She kissed Gus gently on his forehead and walked out the door, disappearing toward the bank of elevators around the corner. "Take care of him for me," she called back to Phyllis again. Her voice cracked, and tears ran down her cheek.

"What did she mean?" Audrey asked after she had gone. "It sounds like she's leaving."

Phyllis didn't know it then, but that was the last she would see of Dr. Lewis. She would ask Gus about her when he woke up. If he woke up.

CHAPTER 25
Phyllis

Phyllis sat with Gus for several hours, hospital staff came and went, water pitchers filled, blood pressure, IVs, temperature, and lot of stuff she didn't have a clue about. She puzzled over Dr. Lewis, who had seemed so dedicated to Gus but left without really saying goodbye to anyone. Gus rolled his eyes a time or two but still hadn't rallied enough to say anything.

Audrey sat with Griff, holding his hand. The swelling had gone down on Griff's foot, and the medical staff put a walking cast on it, but his thinking remained unclear. He called Phyllis *Carlee* once, but no way Phyllis looked like Carlee, and they laughed about how confused he was. He drifted in and out of sleep.

Phyllis had become increasingly curious about Logan and Audrey's relationship. Logan seldom left Audrey's side, and it seemed odd. "I like Logan, Audrey, and he is so attentive to you. Has he ever tried to, you know, I mean, asked you to…?"

"Yes, I like him, too. Tried to what? He's a gentleman, and he's grieving for his wife Joan who died four years ago. Besides I'm with Griff. End of story." Audrey said, shutting Phyllis down. Earlier in the day, she had told Logan that he should vamoose, return to Portland, but after he professed his love for her, she wasn't so sure. But that was for her own knowledge, certainly not for Phyllis'.

Phyllis took Audrey at her word. Carlee had suggested to Phyllis that they were doing the tango or some other dance between the bed sheets on the cruise, but she doubted it because Carlee was the Johnny Appleseed of tall tales. Phyllis did notice that when Logan came into view, she blushed and her eyes sparkled, but that wasn't a sign of an affair.

Audrey and Phyllis had been at the hospital for quite a few hours and both were hungry and thinking about food and drink. Griff had awakened, but remained foggy, and Gus had not yet rallied when Logan appeared and suggested dinner and wine, offering to pay for dinner. Griff growled, "She can pay for her own meal. I'll go with you as I'm hungry, too, and hospital food tastes awful. I'll just take a minute to change clothes. Audrey, help me out of bed."

He maneuvered himself to the edge of the bed and threw his casted leg over the side, its weight threw him off balance, and he twisted and began to slide off the bed. Logan caught him by his shoulder and lifted his foot and torso back on the bed. The sheet fell to the floor, and his derriere hung out of his gown, which made everyone except Griff laugh. Audrey pushed the call button, and a nurse came and injected him with something that made him fall back on the sheets. It looked like he would be sleeping for a while longer.

A bar/restaurant named The Purple Fox sat across the parking lot from the hospital, so Audrey, Logan, and Phyllis headed over, hoping they had a good menu. Logan had called Steve and Carlee saying that Audrey and Phyllis needed support and would be glad to see them. Phyllis puzzled a little more when Logan linked his arm through Audrey's as they left the hospital.

With a name like The Purple Fox, it had to be a welcome distraction. Phyllis and Audrey had read about it in the newspaper and recalled it had a specialty, but, true to form, they had both blocked it out, perhaps a senior moment, and couldn't recall what it was. Senior moments had become increasingly common for both of them, locking tiny bits of information in their brain folds. Audrey and Griff's son Jeff called them brain farts.

The Purple Fox was new to the Hunter bar scene, listing its Pendulum Menu with TBF, traditional bar food, deep fried and greasy, or YBF, yuccie bar food, green and calorie deficient. Phyllis had shared that the term *yuccie*, paralleled the word *yuppie*, but meant *young, urban, creative professionals*, intent on not adhering to their parents' or societal rules. Several artistic posters scattered around the restaurant encouraged *creative autonomy* and *pursue your dreams, at all costs*. Reprints of Diego Rivera, Freda Kahlo, and Picasso's paintings were prominent throughout the bar with a print of Picasso's *Guernica* centered in the room. A large painting of Cole Porter hung next to *Guernica* with the words *Anything Goes* written across the top and *Without Wednesdays* streaming across the bottom. Audrey wondered if it meant they were closed on Wednesdays.

Logan pulled out some bills to pay a cover charge for the three of them, but the doorman in the front of the restaurant waived him off. He attached red plastic bands to Audrey and Phyllis' wrists, and a green one to Logan's. He said, "Unaccompanied ladies are unicorns, and unicorns don't have to pay cover charges, just you, my friend. I believe your friends have already arrived and are waiting for you in the Pendulum Room." He provided each of them with a bar menu and pointed to the room where Steve and Carlee were already seated. Steve said, "I was sorry to hear about Gus and Griff, but, how are they?"

Phyllis started first, "Gus is sedated because they did an ablation, whatever that is, and gave him drugs. They informed me it was a minor heart attack, but it's a wake-up call for both of us. The doctors think he'll be all right, but he'll stay in the hospital for a few days."

Audrey said, "Griff's a mess. He has a broken bone in his foot, an injured knee, injured back and now his head."

Logan interjected, "Don't forget his bunion, but it's much better, I'm happy to report."

"What happened to his head?" Carlee asked.

Audrey related the story about Griff falling off the toilet, adding, "He banged his head, and he seems confused. He has a concussion, but the doc indicated it's minor. He's grouchy and complaining, but he'll be better tomorrow after a good night's sleep and when he goes home. He's okay for the time being, but I'm glad they kept him in the hospital. It's good to see you, and, before I forget, I need a ride home, as I left my car at home when the EMTs transported Griff to the hospital. Could someone drive me home when we finish dinner?"

Logan said, "Actually, we all need rides. None of us has a car. Audrey left hers at home, I had a fender bender and Phyllis' car is on the fritz."

"No problem," answered Steve said, "Carlee and I can take you whenever you're ready."

Steve and Carlee had a drink sitting in front of them and two different platters of food arrived, one with a variety of veggies and sushi and the other heaped with fried food. A third tray held several dips, appropriate for both types of food. Phyllis and Audrey scanned the drink menu and looked at what others were drinking and said, "What's good?"

Logan suggested, "If you want an umbrella drink, which seems to be their specialty, you could try a Barbados Surprise, or you can order a glass of wine. They actually have a decent wine list."

"Wine sounds fine, Pinot Grigio, please," Audrey answered. She dug out her credit card and indicated she'd pay for both.

Phyllis agreed, "I'll have the same."

"Oh, no, ma'am, you are unicorns, so you won't be charged," the waiter responded, smiling. "Unicorns don't pay for anything."

"Why am I a unicorn?" Audrey asked, baffled as to why she had preferential treatment, like free drinks. Griff would be over the top.

"You're a single. Single women are unicorns because they are rare at The Purple Fox. Most people come in pairs, like your friends. Red band means unicorn; green band means leprechaun, playful with a naughty side."

Audrey looked around at Carlee, Steve, and Logan noting the green wrist bands. "I don't understand, but I'm glad to accept a free drink. For the record, though, I am married. My husband just isn't available at the moment."

The server shrugged, "Whatever, Lady, everyone has issues." He left, and Audrey and Phyllis looked at each other and shrugged.

Everyone was quiet for a long minute before Logan suggested, "It would be my guess that we are in a swinger bar."

Audrey had never heard of swinger bars and asked, "What's a swinger bar?"

Logan wrinkled his forehead, "You know, people switching and swapping partners and trying something new. Sometimes group sex, too. I heard of it when Joan and I traveled to Europe a few years ago but didn't realize that Hunter was so hip."

Audrey, looking horrified, exclaimed, "Are you saying this is a bar that allows people to have sex right here. In the bar? I've heard of switching partners and group sex, but not in Hunter, not like this, in a bar. I don't know if we should stay or go." Audrey fell silent as her mind trailed to earlier in the day when she had switched her attention from Griff to Logan. She held her breath, remorseful as she remembered Logan saying, *I love you.* Was she a swinger? she wondered.

Carlee said, "My drink cost $12, so I'm not leaving until I finish it. It's called a Sling-a-pore Swing."

Audrey hoped the others didn't notice her discomfort and forced herself to relax. She looked over the drink menu noting, "I ordered wine, but I will switch later to one of these exotic creations if we stay that long."

A tall athletic woman with red hair that was twisted into a knot walked through the door and tapped Phyllis on the shoulder, "Excuse me, are you A or G." She also had a red band on her wrist. The table grew silent and looked at the woman.

"A or G? What? I'm Phyllis, neither an A nor a G. I guess I'm a P. Audrey starts with an A, but wait! What does it mean?" Phyllis looked to Logan for help.

"A means *all*. G means *girls only*. B means *boys only*. I'm a G and hoped you were, too. Not many unicorns came in today, and I'm looking for a G." She looked at Audrey's wrist and said, "How about you? Are you an A or G?"

Audrey stammered, "N…Neither," and the red-headed woman frowned, turned around, and left the room.

"Now, I need another drink," Logan laughed, as he watched her leave, "and make it a double."

Phyllis commented, "This place is something else. Although I will say that I love the way they have decorated. Of course, I would never engage in swinger sex, although it might be a new and adventurous lifestyle."

CHAPTER 26
Griff

Dinner came and went, and everyone had a second glass of some-thing, talking and laughing about the cruise and life in general. Suddenly, a tray of dishes clattered to the floor, and the muffled din of the restaurant grew to a roar, soon to become a cacophony. People had jumped to their feet, pointing and looking to see what was happening outside the restaurant.

Phyllis heard, "No, sir, you can't go in, I've called the police," and a moment later, blue lights of a police vehicle flickered outside the restaurant.

"My wife's in there. I sure as hell can go in," he roared.

Gus? Had he come across the parking lot?

Phyllis raced to the door, but didn't see Gus, rather Griff standing at the door in his hospital gown that was flapping in the breeze, exposing his backburner for all the world to see. Audrey was right behind Phyllis and cried out, "Griff, no, you should be in the hospital. You are not well, let me take you back to the hospital."

Logan, standing aside Audrey, repeated Audrey's words, adding, "Let me help you."

"You!" Griff shouted, moving toward Logan. "You did this. I was fine until you fixed my bunion, and now, look at me. Quack."

"Griff, Griff, calm down. This is not Logan's fault. It's nobody's fault. It's what happened. Griff didn't cause you to have a bunion. You did that to yourself with poor fitting shoes or when Sadie the cow stepped on your foot last year. Let's go, Hon, back to the hospital," Audrey brushed Logan back as she clasped Griff's arm. "Come on, Hon."

The police carried a blanket from their vehicle and wrapped it around Griff, covering his free-swinging keister, "Sir, let's move you out of the cool air and back to the hospital."

Within a couple minutes, Griff and Audrey sat in the police car on their way back to the hospital. Logan tossed some bills on the table, and he and Phyllis followed the police car across the parking lot.

"How did he get out of the hospital?" Phyllis asked Logan.

"He walked, but it must have been hard between the walking cast and all his other injuries, his back and his knee and his bunion, not to mention his flapping posterior. At least the bunion is better," Logan replied.

CHAPTER 27
Audrey

Logan's description of swingers weighed on Audrey's mind. She had always been faithful to Griff, that's what marriage was about. But then there was Logan. Had she turned into a swinger after one cruise? She had read a few books about sleazy affairs, loving other people, and trying to conceal the tryst from their partners. She had not considered herself in that mode, but the head to toe kiss that Logan had launched had made her wonder because it had been nothing like Griff's kisses. Was she one of those? Was that the definition of a swinger? Was she sleazy? Logan had declared he loved her, and now her brain and heart were at odds with each other. The brain screamed NO, and the heartbeat pounded out YES.

While Griff slept, Audrey continued taking inventory of the good, bad, and ugly of her errant thoughts and activities of late. What would her kids think? She had taught them that marriage was sacred and now, when Griff needed her the most, whoosh, she was swinging away. That *swing* word filled her every thought.

What about Griff? He might be oversexed, but he did not run rampant with other women, at least not that she knew of. Sure, he loved the mating dance, maybe more than most, and even more after he discovered the blue pill and all the other ED drugs on the market, but she was sure he had been faithful. While she wasn't as crazy about sex as he was, she had never denied him, although she admitted she rolled her eyes when he brought up his idea for three-a-days.

What about Logan? He had not been shy about his intentions, making innuendos, hinting, and flirting, and everything he said was kind and pleasant and wonderful. He was romantic, making her feel special and wanted and now, loved. His words *I love you* echoed in her head. Did she love him, too? Did loving two people turn her into a swinger?

Other women had lurid affairs, why not her? What kind of desperation would a person need to have a lurid affair? That was the question of the century. She could count off the emotions about her life in Hunter: Isolation and loneliness topped the list with the next four similar in their effects: boredom, melancholy, seclusion, and now confusion, but what about happiness and joy? And love. They should have been at the top of her list, but they appeared to be crammed in between the couch cushions, grimy and gritty. She had not realized this before, but now it consumed her thoughts. In all these years, she had never acknowledged her emotions because she lived her life one day at a time, accepting the cards she had been dealt and living with the decision she made so long ago. But now, she thought of the trite adage, *two ships passing in the night*, which fit Griff and her lives exactly, dormant and disconnected.

What about her other friends? She would bet that Carlee had played bedroom games with many men. She flirted with a bawdiness that turned Griff and Gus and Steve's faces red. Carlee talked, even bragged about sex and her libido and used words that Audrey had never known to be uttered aloud. She had seen them in books, but they weren't common. At least not to her.

Phyllis, not so much. She was a schoolteacher and loved Gus, and they were one solid item, a team. But Audrey did wonder about the bracelet that Phyllis had cherished and lost. The bracelet contained the names of many countries, *England, Italy, France*, but Audrey had also noticed some men's names, *Omar, Johnny, Miguel*, and they weren't countries, she knew that for sure. She wondered who they were.

CHAPTER 28
Audrey

The doctors recommended that Griff spend two more days in the hospital learning to walk with a cast and a cane and adjusting to a change in medications, which gave Audrey some time to spend alone. Logan, however, didn't see it that way. He rented another car and drove her to the farm. She hadn't been home since Griff's nose-dive off the toilet and she didn't know what condition the house was in, maybe messy, maybe not. Sink would be clogged, she knew that. Logan probably didn't know how to unclog a sink, so maybe Rosemary's son could unclog it while Griff was laid up.

Audrey was apprehensive about Logan's presence at their home, after all, it was Griff's home, too. She wanted to push back, but her body stirred when he was around and when she resisted him, her energy flew out the window. This whole ordeal with Griff, then Gus had worn her out and she didn't have the strength to confront Logan about his presence.

"Let me stay with you, Audrey, I want to be with you, and it wouldn't be good to be alone right now," Logan said.

"I can be alone," Audrey countered. "I've lived in this house many years and know it well. We live so far out in the country that no one would ever bother me. Let's have a glass of wine or something and I'll send you home, back to your room in the hotel." She stopped as she thought of the room in the hotel and the tea cart with food, and flowers, and chocolate, and the words Logan had said to her just a few hours before.

"Is that what you really want, Audrey? Do you want me to leave?

We have hardly been alone from the time we met. So, I am wondering why we couldn't spend some time really talking, thinking, trying to uncomplicate your life? You know that I'm crazy for you, but we should be sure that it is more than a lustful toe fetish. I have never felt this way about anyone, including Joan, and I loved her dearly."

The thought of his hotel room gave her pause, "I don't know," she whispered, "I don't know anything anymore."

Logan rose and immediately spotted a bottle of wine, "You need wine buying lessons, my dear; is this the best you have?" He opened a couple cupboards and drew out another bottle and smiled, "This is more like it; I'll open this one." He rummaged around in a drawer and produced a corkscrew and proceeded to open the bottle.

"Don't make me drunk," Audrey laughed as she sipped her wine. "You are so tempting, and I might remove all my clothes and throw myself at you if I get drunk."

Logan sat down next to her and clasping her hand in his, "Listen, Audrey, drunk or not, I won't violate your honor, as they said in the old days, and I won't let you either. I have too much respect for you to do anything that you might have second thoughts about when you are stone cold sober. I don't want you thinking that I lured you, although luring you, accosting you, making love to you is constantly on my mind. As a matter of fact, you are my mind's lone thought these days, front and center. I can't shake you from my thoughts."

"Logan, I can't…"

"Can't what? Can't be happy? Can't have joy or love? Why not?" He thought about adding the word *sex* but abandoned it.

Did he read her mind? Weren't those the exact words she stated that had been absent from her life. "How did you know…," she began.

Logan interrupted, "I'm not a psychologist or a mind-reader, but you have unhappiness written all over your face. When I look at you and Griff, I see no joy, rather I see tension, not between you and Griff but within yourself. You are unhappy, and all I want to do is please you, to make you happy, to make you love yourself as much as I love you."

CHAPTER 29
Phyllis

The nursing staff allowed Gus to get out of bed the second day after his surgery and he walked to the bathroom and back with Phyllis's help. The surgery frightened her, and she hadn't left his side since she had gone to The Purple Fox, except to visit the hospital cafeteria for salad and bottles of water.

Gus kept his eyes peeled on the door to the room, "Where's Dr. Lewis? She told me she'd be here when I came out of surgery, but I haven't seen her, she hasn't even dropped by to say hello. She was working in the ER, which is just downstairs. Where is she?"

"She left, apparently. Logan and Audrey and I had been all over Hunter trying to find you while she was with you all along. When we finally found you, she kissed you and told me to take care of you and left. She said her calibration system wasn't working but didn't say anything else, and we haven't seen her since. I could check in the ER to see if she's working, because you are right, it's strange that she hasn't come by. If she left Hunter, I'd expect her to say goodbye." Phyllis was as puzzled as Gus. "What was the calibration system, anyway?"

Gus wasn't sure how to answer, after all, the calibration system had been...well, delightful, but Phyllis definitely would not have approved, "It is strange. Why don't you check with the ER to see if she left town?"

"I'm gonna do that," Phyllis agreed. "She mentioned that she wanted to take you to Denver to go shopping and I was about to put my foot down. Her obsession with you and the calibration system, whatever that is, was beginning to frighten me. I was afraid she was going to try to steal you away from me. I'm going to check with the ER and find out where she is. Maybe she's working double shifts or something."

Phyllis went to the ER where she asked for Matt, the RN, but he was nowhere to be seen. An efficient looking nurse's aide walked by and Phyllis flagged her down to ask about Dr. Lewis' whereabouts.

The aide hedged on her question, "Dr. Lewis? Oh, yes, well, I'm not sure, I mean she's gone. She doesn't work here anymore."

"Why not? Do you know where she went? She was helping my husband, Gus, but she left without saying anything," Phyllis asked.

"I don't know if I should say anything, and I don't know much, but I believe she was fired. It seems she was not a doctor after all, but a sex therapist and had been masquerading as a doctor. She had a doctorate degree, but her degree was in sex therapy, not medicine, and she practiced a variety of alternative medicines, most of which had a sexual nature. It might work in some hospitals, but not in Hunter, Idaho."

CHAPTER 30
Audrey

Two days later Griff was ready to go home. He could get in and out of chairs and beds without falling. His meds were stable, and he seemed a little more pleasant. He learned how to use a cane and had mastered the grabber tool, making him less dependent on Audrey.

Audrey had considered Logan's observation that she was unhappy, and she realized that while she might not be unhappy, certainly she wasn't at her happiest. This ordeal had worn her out and just anticipating caring for Griff while he recuperated fatigued her. She knew she needed a break.

A few days after Griff had been discharged from Hunter Hospital, Audrey received a phone call from their two sons in Huckleberry, Oregon, a small city near Portland with a dynamite view of Mount St. Helens.

"Who's on the phone?" Griff growled as she put the phone back in the cradle. He had taken to his wheelchair again because his casted right foot ached, his knee throbbed, and he had back spasms. His bunion had flared up, and he couldn't fit his left shoe on his foot. He wanted a fresh toe splint because the one he had was soiled, but he couldn't drive himself to the store. The toe splint was helping, but he refused to ask Logan.

"Jeff called. He and Lizzy invited me to Oregon to babysit the kids for a week. Lizzy has a week-long conference in Seattle, and Jeff and Mike planned a spring fishing trip, I'm not sure where, maybe Tahoe, and they don't have anybody to watch the kids." Griff and Audrey's sons, Jeff and Mike, lived near each other and usually supported each other's babysitting needs. Huckleberry was situated a few miles west of Portland, where Logan Hall practiced podiatry, but Logan said he had never met them. They weren't old enough for bunions or hammer toes.

"Why do you have to do it? Why can't Abby watch all of them? She's a stay-at-home mom and doesn't do anything," Griff asked. "And who's going to take care of me?" Abby was married to Mike and besides tending to her children, she did yoga and played bridge with her friends. Griff didn't care for Abby much and resented that she stayed home while Mike, a landscaper with his own business, worked twelve-hour days, sometimes seven days a week.

Audrey smiled, "This is the best part, Abby's scheduled to attend a yoga retreat in Denver. I will be able to play with all four of the kids at once, the opportunity of a lifetime. Grandma time!"

"What about me?" Griff repeated. "Who's going to take care of me?"

"Oh, Griff, don't be a baby. I'll only be gone for a week, and I'll ask our friends to look in on you. I'll ask each of them to come by one or two days, so you'll be covered every day; Phyllis and Carlee will check in on you, and Steve will stop by, too. That's what friends are for. Besides, it's too cold to be outside. I'll cook up some food and you can nuke it. Easy peasy. Gus can't help since he is still in the hospital, but Phyllis will help out."

"What about the quack, Logan? Couldn't he stop, too?" Griff's mouth slid into a frown, and Audrey knew he was unhappy.

Audrey was cautious in her next answer, "Maybe. I'll ask him, but you've been rude to him, so I doubt he'll drop by."

"Grandma time? What about grandpa time? You never mention that, and you're abandoning me when I need the most help. By the way, are you and Logan doing the dirty?" Griff asked for the umpteenth time. He already knew what she would say.

"You think that, but we are just friends," she fibbed. "We have the same interests, you know, exercising and eating healthy." Her mind flashed to her time with Logan, *exercising with toe-gasms and the that must have been healthy because she felt good afterwards, like spending a week at a spa.* They had also spent two nights in Griff and Audrey's house last week, but it had been a platonic sleepover, much to Logan's chagrin.

"I don't really like this," Griff said, "you should be staying home. I don't like you driving that far by yourself, and the kids can pay for a babysitter for a week. They both make good money, and Abby could skip her yoga retreat. She doesn't do anything at home anyway. When we will you be back?"

Audrey paused as she thought, *I'm not driving alone, but I'm keeping that a secret,* but she said, "Jeff said they have hotel reservations starting Friday and today is Sunday, so I'll leave tomorrow morning and spend a couple days with Jeff and Mike to learn about the kids' routines and schedules. It's only an eight-hour drive. It'll save them money, and I'm sure you recall how tight money was when our kids were little. Besides that, what can happen?"

CHAPTER 31
Audrey

Audrey fixed Griff's breakfast, pancakes and bacon, hugged him good-bye, and left the house precisely at eight o'clock. She found Logan waiting in front of the hotel with several bags piled in front of him. He said, "Before we leave town, do you mind if we stop at the ski shop because I bought a ski rack and skis for my daughters and I need to attach them to the top of your car. Everything that had the word *ski* in it was on sale, seventy-five percent off or more."

Audrey perked up at the phrase *seventy-five percent off*. "Of course, maybe I should buy skis for the kids, too. Four sets of kids' skis and boots and maybe coats, too. I can shop while you install the ski rack. Because we didn't bring them any presents from Lisbon, skis would be a good idea. How many pairs of skis will fit on your rack?"

"Four, but the kids' skis will fit inside your SUV. I want the ski shop to install the ski rack, so we won't have any problems," Logan said. "It is possible to slide off if it's not installed properly. It won't hurt your car."

Audrey agreed, "While I'm shopping, could you set the car's GPS? You know my technology skills aren't particularly good. I'll buy the skis, and we can buy some snacks, too. Neither of us eats sweets, but I might surrender to a donut and hot cocoa this chilly morning. A drive-in is located across the street from the ski shop, but I'm not sure if they are open at this early hour."

Logan said, "I am delighted that you were able to arrange this trip.

Griff has been so protective of you since we arrived in Hunter that he hardly lets you out of his sight."

"He pitched a minor fit, but since our sons called requesting a babysitter for their kids for a few days, and grandma-time is hard to come by, he didn't argue much. And, I just happened to be available," she explained smiling. "I don't see them often enough, and this is a great opportunity for us all to reconnect. And I want to do some shopping, I plan on buying a new phone. My flip phone is obsolete, and my older two grandchildren can help set up a new one, one of the fancy ones. The X phone or something and I can have them teach me to text and use email and Instant-Gram. And I want to buy Phyllis a Huckleberry charm if I can find one at a jewelry or souvenir store."

"Does Griff know that I am driving with you? I can't imagine he would be happy, in fact, he would be furious," Logan inquired.

She quickly answered, "No, no, no. He doesn't know, and he doesn't need to know. He would be angry, that's for sure. I fixed enough meals for a week, which he can microwave, and I set a visiting schedule for our friends to check on him every day. You know, Day 1: Steve; Day 2: Phyllis, etc. Everybody's on board. Phyllis is the only one who knows you are accompanying me, and she promised she wouldn't tell, and I trust her. Griff has a cell phone, and I put new batteries in the TV clicker. What more could he want? He has the cast on his foot and his back and his knee and bunion haunt him, but he can be miserable all by himself. I bought two bottles of Jack Daniels and two twelve packs of beer, hopefully enough for an entire week even if Steve or someone else shows up."

Audrey paused and frowned, "Griff refuses to go to our primary care doctor and didn't want you to check him out either. He's just being stubborn. Being alone in the house for a few days might be good for him, and maybe he'll start to appreciate me. I'm ready for something different, new and adventurous, as Phyllis says."

As Audrey parked the car, Logan exited and arranged to have the ski rack installed on Audrey's vehicle. It would only take a few minutes, the mechanic promised. Audrey whirlwinded through the store, picking up four winter coats and four sets of skis. Boots were more difficult, because she was unsure of the sizes, so headed to the displays of gloves and hats and tossed several in her cart, as well. Thirty minutes later, the rack and four sets of skis were on the top of the car, the other sets of skis and various items of clothing had been stowed in the rear of the car and they were on their way to Oregon. The drive-in had just opened, and they each bought a sugar donut and hot chocolate.

They settled into the drive and headed for the Interstate. Logan said, "The GPS says four hundred and fifty miles, about seven hours driving time, plus an hour for bathroom breaks, gas, and whatever else comes up, meaning we'll arrive in eight hours, give or take. Do your sons know that you are coming today? Maybe you should give them a heads up."

"No, I told them tomorrow evening, close enough because I might have other things to do," she said with a coy smile.

Logan bit the last of his donut and swigged the hot chocolate, and captured her hand from the steering wheel and began to massage it, "Are you propositioning me?"

"Maybe…"

CHAPTER 32
Phyllis

Gus' doctor wanted to keep him in the hospital for at least another two weeks. Phyllis had been at the hospital for four days and nights, and Gus saw the weariness and worry in her eyes and sent her home. "I love you, Phyllis, but go home, take a break and come back in two or three days after you have rested. I'm fine, but I can see that you aren't because you are exhausted."

Phyllis reluctantly agreed and remembered that she would have to cancel the party and the lobsters. She didn't know where her car was or if it had been fixed. She wanted to stay with Gus, but he was insistent, and she had several things to do at home anyway.

When the Uber arrived at her house, the street was dark and streetlights glowed, but it looked like no one lived there. Vacant. Empty. This was the first time in forty years that she had been without Gus, and the silence reverberated as she stepped into the empty house and onto the hardwood floors. She felt abandoned and alone and flipped on every lamp and light, brightening the rooms, but the emptiness lingered. She wandered through the house, checking the refrigerator and cupboards looking for something or nothing, she wasn't sure which.

She was overcome with sorrow and looked around. Gus was alive, thank heavens, but for now she had no one to talk to and no one to listen or answer. No one to touch, no one to laugh with. Without Gus the house was just a house, no longer a home. It was a cold impersonal building, a hollow chamber. Gus is what made their house a home.

Hoping to fill the silence, she turned on the TV and flipped through the channels. News, history, sitcoms, nothing sparked her interest. And rather than extinguishing the silence, the sounds echoed through the house reminding her of how empty it was, so she switched if off.

She sat down at the kitchen table and poured herself a glass of wine and thought of Gus, alone also, in his hospital bed. She jangled her new bracelet, unpeeled the clasp, and threw it across the room. "What have I done? Gus, Gus, Gus. I will never have another you," she said aloud, as if anyone could hear her.

She thought about the bracelet and all the encounters she had on her trips, as Gus waited for her on the ship, loving her, while she was deceiving him. She thought of Griff and Steve and her lusting of Logan and shook her head. "I'm done," she said aloud.

She knew she couldn't sleep and loathed her infidelity, her lustful thoughts, while she had the best of everything in Gus. Thankfully, she had not lost Gus permanently, but still had to manage her life without him for the time being. She was void of his companionship, communication, and intimacy. The silence was sending a message: Gus. Only Gus. No one else. Although Gus' libido had fizzled of late, she loved his warm, cuddly body to snuggle with as well as his cuddles and coos and even the grunts and groans that sounded in his sleep.

The conspiratorial secrecy that permeates the relationship between a husband and wife had been interrupted and, for right now, she had no one to tease and cajole with the little things in life, like who would fix the coffee or get the mail or take out the garbage. Gus announced that he loved her every day since they met, and she missed him.

Tears rolled down her cheeks as the phone rang. "Hello? Who's this? Oh, hi, Steve."

CHAPTER 33
Audrey

The GPS appeared to be working, but two hundred miles into their trip, Audrey and Logan hit a construction zone forcing them to take a detour, which turned out to be an old logging road, fifty or more miles long with a series of hair-pinned curves though a mountainous pass. The GPS recited *recalculating, recalculating* with every turn, and neither Logan nor Audrey knew how to turn it off, so it continued to bark its orders.

The detour ran north of the freeway, and the weather did not cooperate, mixing rain, sleet, and snow on an already wet and icy road. Visibility was not a problem, but the intermittent patches of ice and snow slowed them down considerably. Logan offered to drive, but Audrey had driven the unpredictable roads in Hunter for many years and shook him off. The speed limit decreased by half, and cars piled up in front of them, all in the same fix, wanting to return to the Interstate as quickly as possible.

Two cars ahead of them, a van unexpectedly screeched to a stop as a deer ran across the road. Audrey slammed on her brakes jostling both of them, stopped her vehicle, and automatically said, "Look for the second one because deer usually travel in mobs of two or more." Audrey was correct and a nearsighted doe miscalculated her distance and ran directly into the side of Audrey's car, splayed its front legs on the car door, and looked Logan directly in the eye. Logan did a double take, but the deer looked even more terrified before reversing itself and sprinting up a hill. Before that deer had left, a six-point buck leapt across the front of the car, and kicked its hoof at their windshield, chipping it, before it stumbled to the ground and grappled to stand before disappearing into the trees. With the freezing weather, the windshield chip spider-webbed, and Audrey's view decreased substantially.

Audrey and Logan, both a bit shaken up, looked at each other. "Did you bring wine?" Audrey asked, "because I could sure use some right now." A few minutes later, they began to descend the mountainous road, and a full-service truck stop appeared. "What do you think? Should we stop? We could continue with our heads stuck out the window if you like," Logan joked.

Audrey pulled into the service lane of the garage and stopped the car but didn't see any attendants until a man strode out of the restaurant and addressed them, "It looks like you two busted a window," he said with a southern Idaho drawl. He turned his head from one way to the other, and said, "I don't know whether we can fix it, but we'll try." He had a large smile with an equally large scar that ran from chin to ear. He told them his name was *Buster* and he would help them. "Why don't you folks freshen up and get a bite to eat while I figure out what your Plan B is. I'll call you on your cell phone after I check the damage. Just leave your keys in the car, and I'll take care of everything." He wrote down Audrey's cell phone number, and Logan and Audrey, leaving their coats in the car, dashed into the truck stop, ready for coffee and food.

Twenty minutes later, Audrey's phone rang, and she answered, hoping it was Buster, but it was a robocall, and they impatiently ordered more coffee and tuna sandwiches. They finished their meal but received no call from Buster and finally returned to the garage to find out how long it would take Buster to replace the windshield.

Logan looked around and said, "I don't see Buster, or your car either."

The service manager, smartly dressed in a blue uniform, wrinkled his brow, "We don't have anybody working here named *Buster*. Are you sure you have the right name?"

"Yes, he told us his name was Buster. He had black hair with a scar on his face. Where's my car?" Audrey asked. "It's a silver SUV with the ski rack on it. And our suitcases are in it, too."

"With the bad weather, we haven't had anybody stop since morning, I'm sorry, I'm at a loss…" The service manager trailed off and interrupted himself saying, "Look, Lady, you've been scammed. When did you say you left it, about an hour ago? It's an hour down the road by now. We've had a series of car thefts in this area, but this is the first one from here. You should file a police report. You can use our phone to call them."

Logan interrupted, "We'll file a police report and also an insurance report, but it's late, and we are on our way to Huckleberry, Oregon. Where can we rent a car?"

"The closest place to rent a car is seventy miles from here, twenty miles or so past the end of the detour. You might want to catch the bus, which should be passing through in an hour, but with the weather as it is, I doubt it will come tonight. There is a small motel on the other side of the restaurant. They are open if they aren't already booked for the night, you can catch the bus in the morning and ride it all the way to Huckleberry because it goes to Portland and Huckleberry is nearby, lucky for you."

"Lucky, my foot," Audrey grumbled. "What time does it arrive in Huckleberry, do you know?"

They called the police and gave a description of Audrey's car, along with a detailed list of what was in it. Audrey was crushed; her grandkids' skis and gear had been stolen, and they were stuck in the middle of nowhere without a change of clothes, or even coats for that matter.

The Hidden Garden Inn sat behind the truck stop with several semis parked in an adjacent lot. Logan held the door for Audrey as they entered the motel. The small lobby consisted of a counter-top desk and a time-worn rust-colored couch and a table stacked with dog-eared magazines. A coffee pot and Styrofoam cups sat on a table against the wall, and since it was late in the day, it emitted a foul coffee smell. A sign over the coffee pot said, "Coffee, fifty cents a cup."

A sign hanging on the wall listed their prices: Hourly rate: Singel $10.00, Dubl $12.00. Logan asked for a room on the first floor.

"How many hours do you want it for?" the clerk asked. "It's twelve bucks an hour with clean sheets; nine for hot cots."

"All night, clean sheets. We're taking the morning bus," Logan answered. He handed the man his credit card and signed for the room. He had never stayed in a by-the-hour motel before and was surprised they accepted credit cards.

"Do you want towels?" Horse-face asked. "Bath size, two bucks, hand towels, one buck, washcloths, half a buck."

Logan looked at Audrey, smiled and said, "What do you think, Baby? Shall we shoot the wad and rent some towels and washcloths, too?"

"Yes, let's do. Two bath size and two hand towels, no washcloths. I'll pay for those," Audrey replied pulling six dollars from her purse. Her by-the-hour motel experience was sorely lacking as well.

Horse-face said, "That's the rental fee, and you can't keep them." He handed Audrey four thread-bare towels that had been once white, but now tinged yellow-grey. Made of terry cloth, they should have been soft, but the frequent washings and bleaching made them as scratchy as burlap.

The motel room was exactly as Logan and Audrey had envisioned it, small, dank, and cold. Logan switched the broken heater dial to high and it sputtered and crackled, making Logan skeptical of whether it worked or not. As promised, it was seemingly clean, although it had well-used sheets that smelled like bleach from three feet away. Audrey wondered how she would ever sleep in them. A small desk holding a 1980's vintage TV and two frayed, webbed aluminum lawn chairs made up the rest of the room's ambiance. Besides bleach, the room smelled of unidentifiable odors of the hundreds of weary travelers who had come before them.

The bathroom didn't hold much promise either. The 1950's lime green washbasin and pink tiled shower with gray grout contrasted with the whitish toilet with a brown ring, which gurgled and belched when flushed. The rusted shower curtain with missing rings sagged over the toilet making it difficult to use the facilities. Logan could not quite reach the curtain rod, so he balanced himself on the side of the bathtub and stretched upward. He started to topple and grabbed the rod, which crashed to the floor pulling him with it, sprawling him half in and half out of the bathtub. The shower curtain ripped into two pieces and covered his face and upper body. Opposing scents of Lysol and grime filled his nostrils, and he swatted it like a fly attempting to remove it from his person. Desperate to get it off him, he shouted for Audrey.

Audrey sped into the tiny bathroom to help him, but in his effort to free himself, he had encased himself even more in the grimy curtain. She tugged and pulled at what seemed to be a decade's old curtain, unable to free it. Logan grabbed her arm and inadvertently pulled her into the bathtub headfirst. She scrambled to get out of the tub and slid to the floor and needed to leverage herself with the toilet in order to stand. Logan, sprawled in the tub, freed himself from the curtain, and threw it to the floor, rolled over to his knees and with her help, stepped out of the tub. She assisted him to one of the aluminum chairs, and he sat down, but the frayed webbing jerked and one strand broke and dumped his butt three inches below the aluminum frame.

"Dang, Audrey, this is a disaster. I never thought I'd say it, but I'll be glad when that bus appears tomorrow."

Audrey said, "That's okay, there's no way I would take a shower in there. All I can think about is The Bates Motel. I don't even know if I can sleep in that bed. Oh, Logan, how bad is this motel?"

Logan, who was accustomed to upper scale everything, said, "It's the worst motel I've ever seen or even knew existed. I'd rather be sleeping outdoors in the snow with that deer that stared me in the eye. Let's go back to the truck stop and see what type of alcohol we can find, hopefully something stronger than beer. At this point, I don't really care what it is. How much worse can things be?"

They returned to the truck stop, and before they went into the dining area to eat, Audrey pulled Logan aside and pointed to a rack of jackets and sweatshirts. "We left our coats in the car, so I'm going to buy a sweatshirt. It's cold now and bound to be colder in the morning." The rack had a limited variety of sweatshirts, all of which seemed sun-bleached and dingy, but they settled on matching hooded sweatshirts saying *Truckstop Tourist* and picturing a gasoline pump. They each bought a ball cap with the same logo. "A remembrance of times past," Logan said with a chuckle.

"Fitting," Logan said as they sat down in one of their plastic booths, predictably adorned with black electric tape. With wine and beer listed as the only available alcoholic drinks, they ordered two red wines each and gulped one down before they decided that they might as well order dinner. The waitress apologized that they didn't have any wine glasses, and served the wine in water glasses, filled to the brim. She put a slice of lemon on the rim of each glass, *for looks*, she said.

Logan ordered the special of the day, which was chicken fried steak with mashed potatoes and gravy, and Audrey ordered a hamburger and fries. "What can they possibly do to ruin a hamburger and fries?" she asked. As her food arrived, her phone rang, and things grew worse, "It's Griff," she whispered.

CHAPTER 34
Audrey

Griff's voice boomed on the other end of the line, "Audrey, it's me, Griff, where are you? Are you okay? The state police called informing me that they have our car and want to know what to do with it. What's going on?"

"Oh, Griff, I'm okay. It's awful," Audrey explained, "A deer hit us, and another one shattered the windshield, and a guy named Buster stole our car, and now we're at this horrible motel with lawn chairs and a pink shower without a shower curtain."

Logan grimaced as she spoke to Griff because he heard the *us* and *we're*. He shook his head at her, but she didn't catch it. Griff did though.

"Who are you with, Audrey? Who's the *us* and *we're*? Are Jeff and Mike with you? Are you already in Huckleberry? They can help you with the car. Let me talk to one of them," Griff ordered. "Put Mike on."

Audrey stopped talking and looked at Logan with moon eyes knowing she had been caught and knew she would have to manufacture an alternative story. "No, I'm not in Huckleberry and Jeff and Mike are not with me. Don't blow a gasket, but on the way out of Hunter, I stopped at the ski shop and bought some ski stuff for the kids because it was seventy-five percent off. Logan happened to be at the ski shop, we talked, and he asked if he could tag along to Huckleberry, because it's close to his Portland home. You said you worried about my driving alone, and I had plenty of room, so I couldn't see any reason he couldn't. I didn't tell you because I knew you would have either thrown a fit or wanted to come, and you are too injured to make the trip. Logan purchased skis for his daughters and a ski rack, which we attached to the roof of the car." Most of this was the truth, and she felt confident about what she said, so far.

"So, you're with Logan? Are you and he staying at a motel? I guess I'm glad you are not alone, but I don't like this one bit, Audrey," Griff growled.

The truck stop dining area was crammed and noisy, but she filled him in as much as she dared. "Yes, a guy pretended to be a mechanic offering to fix the windshield, but he stole our car instead, and now we are stuck at this awful motel called the Hidden Garden Inn, but don't worry, we have separate rooms. Right now, we are eating dinner at the truck stop. Logan's eating a CFS and I have a burger and fries, extra ketchup. We're okay, Griff, and before you ask, I'm not doing the dirty with him. Where's the car?" She wanted to change the subject before she made another error. "We hoped to take a bus to Huckleberry tonight, but the weather is so bad that the buses stopped running. The storm should clear out by morning, and we can take the morning bus. When we arrive in Huckleberry, I'll call you and send Jeff and Mike back for the car."

Griff was ranting and swearing when they ended the call, and Audrey said, "We could write a book about this trip. It is one to remember. I just hope Griff doesn't kill one or both of us. He was livid."

"The room should be warm by now. I'll buy a box of wine and beg two Styrofoam cups to put us out of our misery for tonight."

CHAPTER 35
Audrey

Although they snuggled together, sleep on the lumpy bed did not bring rest to either Audrey or Logan. The heater hissed and sputtered throughout the night, turning itself off when it reached a certain temperature, and loudly restarting when the room cooled.

Logan set the alarm for seven, knowing the bus should be rolling through at eight-thirty, but they both spilled out of bed before six o'clock. Audrey looked at their slept-in, wrinkled clothes and was thankful for the steam iron she found in the makeshift closet. She plugged it in, hoping to make herself more presentable. While she waited for the iron to heat, she dampened one of the dollar hand towels and washed her face and hands in the lukewarm water with the minuscule soap bar. She considered rubbing her teeth with the towel but thought better and abandoned that idea. Maybe the truck stop would have a toothbrush.

The iron had heated up nicely when she tested it with a damp finger. She had set it on medium-high and it hissed, and steam rolled out of the top. *Thank heavens, it works.* She rolled the iron over the ironing board and it worked fine. Ten minutes and she'd be done. She placed her corduroy slacks on the board and smoothed them over. The same with her cotton sweater. *Piece of cake.* Logan had worn a pair of wool-blend slacks and matching sweater, so she lowered the temperature to its lowest setting, waited until it cooled, and began stroking the sweater's sleeve, not realizing it contained a synthetic fiber that shriveled with heat. "Oh, no, not now," she screamed as the sleeve began to shrivel and turn brown.

Tears rolled down her cheeks as she began peeling the cloth from the iron, "Oh, Logan, I'm so sorry. Does this have a nylon fiber in it?"

Logan shook his head. "What a trip. It's like a *National Lampoon* movie. One thing after another. I'll wear them as they are. It's just the sweater sleeve, so no real harm was done. I'm glad you didn't start with the pants. A shriveling crotch might have made quite a statement," he laughed. "I can cover the sweater with my spiffy new Truckstop Tourist sweatshirt."

"Let's go eat breakfast but unplug the iron before we go. With our luck, we would burn the place to the ground."

The bus appeared on time, and both were relieved to be on the road. They found seats near the middle of the bus and snuggled together for the ride to Huckleberry. Soon its gentle sway and drone put them both to sleep. It had been years since either of them had ridden a bus, but they found it clean and comfortable, far superior to the previous night's accommodations.

The bus stopped for a food and bathroom break every two hours, the first being outside a truck stop a few miles from the Idaho/Oregon border. They stretched and exited the bus for their forty-minute stop and bought their second coffee and donut in twenty-four hours. They walked around the rest area when Logan said, "Audrey, that's a State Police office. Isn't that your car in front? It sure looks like it. We have twenty minutes until the bus starts up again, so let's go see."

They increased their pace, and in less than a minute stood in front the station beside Audrey's car. "Hallelujah! Our luck is changing, except that the skis, ski rack, and all the presents I bought the kids are gone. Our suitcases are gone, too," Audrey exclaimed as they stormed through the door to the station.

"Who cares?" Logan returned. "We are safe, and your car appears intact. Let's go!"

Thirty minutes later, papers signed, and thanks all around, Audrey and Logan jumped in the car ready to go to Huckleberry. Another thirty minutes and the windshield had been replaced.

CHAPTER 36
Audrey

The sun glared in their eyes as they drove west to Huckleberry, a few miles from Portland, but they could easily admire Mount St. Helens to the north, majestic and snowcapped with trees as far as they could see. Later in the year beneath the trees, huckleberries grew, sweet and juicy. Logan and Audrey had crossed the wild and free Deschutes River that roared high and loud this time of the year as the snowcapped mountains thawed, and the snow flowed into the main river.

They were both relieved to be nearing their destination. The trip was nearly a day longer than they anticipated, but they were fine, sans skis and presents. Their cell phones were both drained and of no use, but Logan remembered he had chargers at home.

Logan had driven the last hundred miles and slowed as they entered Huckleberry, which was about twenty miles from his home in Portland. Logan said, "I haven't been home for nearly two years, and it appears that Huckleberry has growing pains. Joan loved Huckleberry and wanted to move here, as she thought it was just the right size of a town. Ample services and things to do, but cozy enough that people knew and cared about each other. I'm already seeing lots of new buildings and street names that I've never heard of before. It's amazing what can happen in two years."

After Joan had died, Logan had remained in Portland two more years and became its most eligible bachelor, even though he was well over the age of Social Security. Women flocked to him, but he had rebuked his many suitors, referring to them as albino cougars since most had white hair. He complained that most wanted him to be their nurse or were after his purse, and the rest sought his community status. He had no interest in any of them.

Logan glanced over at Audrey, admiring her loveliness and complexity. He reflected on the first few minutes that he had seen Audrey standing in the hotel lobby, looking as lost as a chick that had fallen from its nest. Joan was straightforward, kind, and caring, but Audrey was different, simultaneously sophisticated and innocent, both in and out of love with her husband of many years, romantic and sexy, and he hoped she would be willing to take a chance with him. Last night had been challenging, but she had weathered it well. She seemed a little melancholy, but her vulnerability, coupled with her strength, made her even more desirable. Maybe she was in love with him, too. Besides her ironing skills, he knew that he was head over heels in love with her.

He had considered giving up on her while in Hunter, as he couldn't see a future with her in that small town. Griff was a problem and so was Phyllis, for that matter, as she had twice tried to seduce him, and he was flattered. But he had fallen in love with Audrey, not Phyllis.

He wanted Audrey more than he had ever wanted anybody. He didn't know how far their relationship would go, but the night at the Hidden Garden Inn had clarified his emotions and maybe these days together would confirm their destiny. When she was in sight, or even in his thoughts, his ability to control his sexual organs plummeted to zilch.

Twenty miles farther, he headed through a gated community with large lots and expansive houses. "Here we are, home sweet home," Logan said, as he parked in the driveway of a pale yellow two-story colonial home that sprawled across the fenced yard. Attached to the center of the house, two one-story wings doubled the size of the house. One wing held the garage, the other, a sunroom. Full-sized porches with six pillars extended across the front of house on two levels, and windows with shutters sat both top and bottom.

"It's beautiful," Audrey said aloud. "What a gorgeous home and property."

"Yes, it is. Joan designed it, and we built it shortly before she died. She barely lived in it, and the inside still has some gaps that need to be addressed. After she passed away, I had neither the heart nor the time to make it as beautiful as she planned. I decided to travel instead. Let's go in."

They entered, and he walked through the house turning on lamps and opening doors. He turned the heat up before proceeding through the entire house looking in every room. "Nothing seems amiss, but this house depresses me. Joan wanted it badly, so I built it for her, but she died before we could enjoy it at all. It was never really mine and, as it turned out, wasn't hers either. Let's have some wine before we go out to eat. It was a long ride, and the refrigerator is empty, so we'll have to go out to dinner. And maybe we can shower and change clothes, too."

Logan went in search of a bottle of wine and some glasses while Audrey waited in the living room thinking about Logan and their relationship. *This is a lovely house, and he is a lovely man, so different from Griff. He is a real gentleman who seems to be interested in me, but why? He is complex, sexy, and romantic, and at the same time, corny, sentimentally corny. The whipped cream. The toe massages. So silly, but I've learned that I like them. Just thinking about them makes my lower parts gurgle. Griff would have thought them meaningless because he wanted sex, pure and simple. Raw, passionate sex.*

Last night was difficult, but even in the seedy motel in the middle of nowhere, Logan treated me with kindness and love. I scorched his sweater and we both were able to laugh about it.

Logan is handsome with a softness about him. Griff is handsome, too, but in a different way, rugged and dependable. Logan is refined, smooth, almost too smooth. He is a doctor, a widower, the father of two adult girls, and sitting here in his house, I know he's for real. I wasn't sure before. But now that I know, I will soon need to decide. Griff or Logan.

CHAPTER 37
Audrey

"Where shall we go to dinner?" Logan asked. "We could go to a *stander-upper*, meaning a fast-food restaurant, or do you prefer slow and leisurely. You choose. High end, stander-uppers or something in between?"

Audrey laughed, "That's a funny way to categorize restaurants, but something in between sounds best. We've been riding all day, and maybe we could eat a little, then take a walk to wear off the calories and shake out the wrinkles. Are any of the middle contenders close enough to walk?"

"The one I like, called the Vertigo, is about fifteen miles, but they have great food, and Joan and I ate there often. It's worth the drive. You don't have a change of clothes, which sounds wonderful to me, your naked body turns me on, but restaurants have rules about that sort of thing. You can borrow something from one of my daughters or Joan…you are about the same size, or we can go shopping first."

"I think it might be awkward to wear something of Joan's. But if your daughters have something I could borrow, and you are sure they won't mind, that would be great. I can shop tomorrow," Audrey told him.

"I understand, just check their closets. Jan's room is the first one, Laura Lee's is the second. The bathroom is a Jack and Jill, between the two rooms, at the front of the house. Take your time. By the way, the towels will cost you four bucks, two bucks for hand towels, and a buck fifty for a washcloth," he joked. "Wasn't that something? It was the first time I ever had to rent towels at a motel."

"Your towels are lot more expensive than those at the Hidden Garden," she laughed. "I should call Griff to let him know that we arrived, but my phone is dead. I guess I'll wait until after it's charged, and we have eaten dinner. I'm sure he's gonna have a lot of questions. I want to find out if he fixed something for dinner and if Steve showed up. Today's Steve's day to see Griff," Audrey continued.

"Sounds good, finish your wine, and we'll head out. The Vertigo has good food, steak, seafood, salads, anything. I like their steak, but everything else is good, too. And their prices are okay, as well," Logan commented.

Audrey rummaged through the girls' closets that were filled with barely worn clothes, most of which had designer labels on them. She found wool slacks and a blue cashmere sweater with three-quarter sleeves, and thirty minutes later they were on their way. They drove Joan's Lexus, which had been parked in the garage for two years, but it started right up after a cough, a grind, and a sputter, and began to purr, which brought a smile to Logan's face. "I didn't think it would go," he said. "Two years is a long time to sit and wait."

The Vertigo, five miles east of Huckleberry, was filled with music, noise, and laughter, as well as wonderful aromas of bread and beef, and Audrey absorbed the ambiance and aromas. Although Mike and Jeff had lived in Huckleberry for several years, she had visited only three times before and had never been to any of its restaurants. Griff resisted visiting Huckleberry as he preferred that their families visit them in Hunter where they could fish or hunt. Central Oregon also had lots of hunting and fishing opportunities, but Griff liked what he knew.

As soon as they walked through the door, the noise changed, a din, a quiet buzz, as patrons turned to look at them. Logan, prominent in the community, had been absent two years, and his sudden appearance, even at a restaurant, surprised people. Several people rose to greet him, embracing and hugging him, asking him about his trip and when he had returned. They eyed Audrey and nodded at her, but no one said anything. A few seconds later, the hostess seated them at a table for two, and brought them water and menus, as well as a drink menu.

Logan ignored the drink menu and ordered from memory. He named off a red wine that Audrey had never heard of. A bottle arrived moments later, and people continued to greet him as they sipped their drinks and waited for their meals. Logan introduced a few people, quietly admitting to Audrey that he had forgotten his patients' names and referred to them as their foot malady. "He's gout, and what a case! She's heel spur, and it was bad, couldn't wear shoes. He's bunion, worse than Griff's, but I fixed it." He remembered whatever foot problem they had, and it made her laugh.

"By what foot problem would you call me?" she asked when the flow of former patients slowed down.

"Toe-gasm, you would be toe-gasm," he flirted as he squeezed her hand under the table.

They had just ordered dinner when a noisy group with children entered, and Audrey turned as she heard, "Mom! When did you arrive? Where's Dad? Who is this?"

CHAPTER 38
Steve

Steve had been driving by Phyllis' house every day since Gus had his heart attack, hoping to find her home and repeat their time on the cruise ship. He knew that Gus was still in the hospital and thought he might catch her tonight. He enjoyed everything about her. She was sexier, funnier, and had more charisma than Carlee, and if Carlee and Gus weren't in the way, he would think seriously of a permanent hookup. As it is, he thought, a few minutes here and there would have to do. With Gus in the hospital, this was perfect.

He knocked on the door, and she opened it, "Hi, Steve, I just got home, but you can come in if you'd like."

"Hi, Pretty Lady, I'm glad to see you. I've missed you." He leaned over and planted a kiss on her cheek. I was passing by and noticed your lights burning. Would you like company for a little while?"

Phyllis blurted out, "Yes, I'm here." She choked back her tears, realizing her vulnerability. Two minutes ago, she was regretting her betrayal and now Steve shows up at her door, and she invites him in. What was she thinking? "He's a friend, that's all, a friend," she muttered to herself. "I'll offer him a glass of wine and send him home. Nothing will happen."

Steve was carrying a bottle of wine. "How's Gus? Carlee was talking about going to see him, but I don't think she has yet. He's not home yet, is he? When does he get out of the hospital?"

"The doctors haven't said yet, maybe another week," Phyllis answered thinking, *he brought wine, this might be difficult.*

"I have new hearing aids," Steve said, patting his pocket. "I just got them but haven't put them in yet. I should be able to hear everything now. I purchased them from the new company on Locust Street. They are right here" as he shoved them in his ears. "Do you want to see them?"

Phyllis didn't know why he would ask her that, "No, thanks, but it's nice to see you, Steve."

"I brought you a bottle of wine. You look like you've been crying, Phyllis, is everything okay, with Gus, I mean?"

"No, he's okay, I'm melancholy, that's all. And lonely. This is the first time Gus and I have been separated for more than a few hours since we've been married. We lived together, taught together, traveled together, and have continually been a part of each other's lives, and now, I don't know what's going to happen. He's doing okay, but it's scary."

Steve put his arm around her and hugged her hard, "I'm here, Phyllis. You don't have to be lonely. Would you like me to stay with you tonight? I'll call Carlee and tell her about how you feel, and she'll be okay. She's worried about you, too. Let me open this bottle of wine."

Phyllis was flustered. *Stay the night? A fun tryst is one thing, but staying the night?* "I just poured myself a glass," she said, "but I'll find another glass, and we can finish off this bottle." Whatever he wanted, and she was sure she knew, would have to wait. Did you come to see Gus?"

As a deep whistle emerged from one of his hearing aids, he yanked them both out rendering him deaf once again. Mis-hearing that Phyllis was asking about Gus, he answered, "Between us, of course, this will be between us. I've missed you and have been thinking of you a lot," Steve's hearing situation yielded a double whammy because not only was he deaf, he barely listened. Without his hearing aids, the conversations didn't go in a logical direction. Clearly, they were not traveling on the same wavelength, not even in the same general direction.

He pulled her close and back walked her into her bedroom. Phyllis' heart skipped a beat, she and she felt some tingles, and was tempted, but Gus. She resisted, sort of, as he kissed the top of her out-of-control mop. Her mind was on Gus, but Steve's mind was on her. They had not crossed paths since they had returned from their trip and he was a welcome sight, but not right now.

"I can't, Steve, now is not a good time. Don't you remember? Gus had a heart attack," she said. "A heart attack."

He pulled away from her and opened his eyes wide. "Gus had a shark attack? Where did the shark come from? We don't have sharks in Idaho. At least not that I'm aware of. Where? The Snake River is loaded with sturgeon and other big fish, but certainly no hospital sharks."

"Heart. Attack. He had. To go. To the Hospital," She repeated slowly, one word at a time.

"He needed his pistol to shoot the shark. I understand, sort of, but not really, you aren't making much sense, Phyllis."

CHAPTER 39
Audrey

Audrey's kids showing up at the same restaurant at the same time could not have been a bigger coincidence nor cause her more distress. She had arrived a day early, not with Griff, rather with a man whom her family knew nothing about. Never heard of him, had no idea who he was, or how he had attached himself to their mother.

Audrey released Logan's hand and jumped to her feet to hug everybody, gathering them into her arms, and repeated her embraces. She teased, "I warned you kids to stop growing, and you didn't. Now two of you are taller than I am, and you two little guys will be taller than I am by tomorrow morning, I'm sure." It had been several months since she had seen them and now two emotions skyrocketed to her heart, pleasure and panic, pleased to see her family, yet terrified of how they would react to her being here with Logan, not their father.

She had often complained about having become invisible, as happened to women of a certain age, but she was not invisible now. Now that she needed invisibility, it had vanished into the clouds. She was elated to stand front and center facing her family yet frightened beyond words. They didn't say anything, just swiveled their heads toward Logan. Unfortunately, he wasn't invisible either and all sixteen eyes focused on him.

Jeff repeated, "When did you arrive? Where's Dad?"

"Who are you?" Mike accused.

She started to answer, but her tongue became tangled up with the foot that was squarely in her mouth. She had anticipated having some time to sort through the predictable questions, but that wasn't working out so well. They wanted to know the answers now, not tomorrow, and they probably had more questions than she had answers, at least answers that she was willing to share.

"Your dad is fine, mostly," but couldn't conjure up the words to explain what *mostly* meant, because Griff wasn't fine, and she was here.

Logan to the rescue. He stood up and said, "I'm Logan Hall, from Portland. Your mother was kind enough to drive me home. We met on the cruise and struck up a friendship. Since she was coming here to see you and babysit, I bummed a ride. End of story."

"Yes, end of story," Audrey stammered, knowing it was not quite the end of the story, barely the beginning, but she hoped it would do for now.

"So, where's Dad?" Mike persisted while looking at Logan. "Didn't he want to come with you?"

"It's a long story which I will tell you, but why don't we feed these hungry kids first, and I can fill you in later? I swear you kids have grown a foot and I'm sure you are starving," Audrey said, eagerly changing the subject. She gathered her four grandchildren into her arms, barricading herself from her sons' inevitable curiosity.

Logan flagged the maître de and requested a table for ten and a postponement of their order so the whole crew could eat together.

CHAPTER 40
Audrey

Dinner struck a silent note with everyone pretending happiness and pondering what came next, as well as what had already happened. Logan and Audrey had experienced two long, tiring days, but had been excited about the prospects of uninterrupted time together, but when Jeff and Mike and families showed up unannounced, their thoughts of heating up suddenly cooled off.

A constant stream of diners continued to greet Logan as they entered or exited the restaurant, welcoming him back to Huckleberry, thanking him for services he rendered years before. Audrey's sons didn't know him, and their curiosity grew. Obviously popular and friendly to his former patients, he had impacted many people's lives, but they had questions. Nobody was asking, and Mom wasn't telling.

Logan ordered another bottle of wine, the same as he had ordered before and added some sparkly stuff for the kids.

Mike, the older of the two with the oldest child syndrome of being in charge, broke the ice, "So, Mr. Hall, how did you meet Mom?" Like Griff, he was cynical and skeptical. His eyes focused on Logan's eyes, casting darts directly at him.

Audrey answered, "He told you, we met on the cruise, and he's Dr. Hall, a podiatrist who lives in Portland. All these people greeting him are former patients."

Mike's darts grew larger, and he now threw daggered stares at Logan, "Okay, Dr. Hall, did you go on the cruise alone?"

Logan paused for a moment before saying, "My name is Logan, please call me Logan. Yes and no, you see, I met your mom and dad and their friends, and we banded together. Being alone on a cruise is no fun, but they kindly adopted me, and I was no longer alone. I liked them all, but your mom and I had a lot in common, and Phyllis, one of our friends, tagged us as BFFs. Best friends forever."

Audrey smiled at Logan as she thought about the other text-talk term of endearment, FWB, but that was another thing her kids didn't need to know. She said, "You remember your English teacher, Mrs. Gustafson, Phyllis Gustafson, that's who he's talking about."

"I remember her and Mr. Gustafson, too," Jeff said. "They were both a lot of fun. Mrs. G sometimes teased the senior boys with flirty innuendos, which made us laugh." Jeff changed the subject back to Logan, "Tell us about yourself, Dr. Logan, do you have family in the area?"

"No, not anymore because my wife died, and our daughters live in the Big Apple. My wife was a pediatrician, maybe you knew her, Dr. Joan Sullivan," Logan answered, shifting his eyes to their children.

"Your wife was Dr. Sullivan? She was our kids' pediatrician, but when she died, two or three years ago, it was a huge loss for us," Mike's wife Abby said. "I liked her a lot, and I'm sorry she died. I didn't know she was married, though."

"She was our pediatrician, too," Jeff's wife, Lizzy said. "She was an amazing doctor."

"Four years. She died four years ago," Logan corrected.

Jeff, more like Audrey, was social, liked people, enjoyed laughter and sought out fun. He reversed the conversation from Logan to Griff, "I'm glad you are here, Mom, but I'm wondering about Dad. First, he had a painful bunion, and later he hurt his back and his knee, but how is he really? You didn't explain much."

Audrey replied, "Well, you know your father, the man in charge of everything, but it got the best of him. I didn't tell you about his latest injury."

"What other injury? What did he do this time?" Mike asked.

"It's classic Dad," I continued. "He fell off the toilet and broke a bone in his foot."

"It was his fibula." Logan corrected.

Jeff started to laugh, "How did he fall off the toilet? I don't know how anybody could fall off a toilet, but if anyone could, Dad would be the guy. Is he okay?"

"He's doing okay, but it was frightening, a story in itself, because he was sitting on the toilet watching me put out a fire that he had started, and he just fell off. Head-first, landing on his face and his belly. I was busy with the fire so didn't really see him fall, just a thump and voila! There he was, spread eagle on the floor, naked as a new-born calf. He hit his head and knocked himself out and broke a bone in his foot. The fibula, as Logan said. He was a sight to behold," I explained.

"Grandpa did that?" the kids chirped in simultaneously as they began to giggle. "He was naked?"

Logan began laughing, too. "You told me he fell off the toilet, but you didn't mention the fire or the lack of clothes. It must have been a sight."

Mike's face began to redden. "Mom, you had a fire and didn't tell us? How much of the house burned?"

"Dad tipped over a candle, and it burned a towel. It was nothing, really. No real damage," Audrey clarified.

"This gets better and better," Jeff commented. "He's not growing old gracefully. If he's not careful, he'll end up in a gray-care facility. He must have been well enough that you could leave him, right, Mom? Can he survive without you? Who's taking care of him? Did you put him in an assisted living while you are gone?"

"Don't worry, he'll be fine. He has a TV remote, beer, and people are checking on him every day. He would have liked to have come, too, I'm sure, but the wheelchair made it too difficult, and all your bedrooms are located on the second floor. Besides, I need a break from his crankiness." Guilt set in, and she wondered if she was being too cavalier. Maybe she shouldn't have left him.

Lizzy asked, "So, Mom, you can stay with us, but where are your car and suitcase?"

The tricky part came next. Audrey had every intention of staying with Logan for the night, but what would her kids say? And would they report everything to Griff before she had a chance to report it herself?

Again, Logan threw her a lifeline. "Her car is at my house in Portland. We need to have it checked out. A deer hit the car and shattered the windshield, but we replaced the glass. I'm going to have my local mechanic take a look, too, to be on the safe side."

"You mean you hit a deer? That can be scary. They can do a world of damage," Jeff pointed out.

Logan answered, "No, a deer hit us, two actually. The first tried to jump the car and ended up staring me in the face. The second, a huge buck, leapt over the car and kicked in the windshield. We fixed the windshield, but our suitcases and some other stuff were stolen at the garage. We got the car back, but it's a mess, so I'll have her car cleaned up and your mom can buy some clothes. I'll take her to the mall, and she will be ready to report for Grandma duty on Friday morning. We came earlier than you expected because she's never seen Mount St. Helens, so we can wake up early and take a little spin to the mountain." Logan didn't know if she had seen Mount St. Helens or not, but he hoped the kids bought it.

CHAPTER 41
Jeff and Mike

That night the sons and their wives huddled up to unravel their suspicions about their mother and her *friend* Logan Hall. They snipped and sniped about him, never heard of him, his wife was dead, and Mike was highly suspicious.

Mike: She's doing him. She left Dad when he had a whole bunch of injuries. She just went off and left him. Stupid old people, anyway. She's totally doing him.

Lizzy: No way. You heard what she said, they are BFFs.

Mike: Did you see how he looked at her? He smiled at her.

Lizzy: Smiling at someone doesn't mean they're doing it.

Abby: I think he's nice, a lot nicer to her than Griff. He can be harsh.

Jeff: She's our mother, no way is she doing it. No way because she's crazy for Dad and would never cross him. Do you remember how she said *till death do us part* is a commitment, not a suggestion?

Lizzy: Well, you know OPTD. They're crazy.

Abby: What's OPTD mean?

Lizzy: OPTD. Old People These Days. Your mom might be having an MC, midlife crisis. Maybe she became tired of your dad being so rude.

Mike: He's not that bad, but I am worried about him. One of us needs to go to Hunter, see Dad, and find out what's really happening. And find out about this Logan guy?

Jeff: Who? We're supposed to go fishing in Tahoe. She's gonna babysit.

Lizzy: He can't be that bad, he was married to Dr. Joan, I liked her.

Abby: Me, too. She was a great doctor.

Mike: She can still babysit. She's here with her *friend* Logan. We'll take our poles and go fishing in Hunter. We won't tell her; we'll just go to Hunter, see Dad, and fish for two things, fish and the truth. Lizzy and Abby can go to their conferences, and we'll stay in Hunter for the entire week. Fishing is good in the spring.

Jeff: You don't think she's telling the truth?

Mike: Do you?

Jeff: I don't know. It does seem a little fishy.

Mike: Maybe we shouldn't leave her here with her *friend*. I mean we know nothing about him, and he could be an axe murderer, for all we know.

Jeff: No, I agree with the girls, he's a doctor, was married to Doctor Joan. He's not an axe murderer.

Mike: That's his story, but I say we can't leave her alone with him.

Jeff: We asked her to babysit the kids and now somebody has to babysit her. This is upside down.

Lizzy and Abby started to laugh.

Lizzy: She's fine; she can take care of herself. And who cares if she's having a little fling? She's earned it. Fifty years on a farm eighteen miles out of Hunter, I'd do it, too. It's sweet, like a quirky half-romance and half-horror story, Grandma runs off with another man leaving Grandpa battered and beaten. Abby, Jeff, and Lizzy laughed again. Only Mike was silent.

Jeff: She'll be fine. Leave her alone. She'll take good care of the kids and we can all have a little vacation. Why don't we all go to Hunter? We'll tell the neighbors to check in on Mom and the kids…they'll be fine.

Abby: Good idea, I'd like to go. I'll pull out of the yoga retreat. Can you ditch your conference, Lizzy?

Lizzy: My boss won't care.

Mike: No question about it. I'm going. I want to get to the bottom of this Logan thing.

CHAPTER 42
Audrey

Audrey and Logan returned to Logan's home and settled in with a brandy night cap. Audrey's head was spinning with anxiety, fear, excitement, and now alcohol. "We should have ordered a take-out dinner, or covered our heads with paper bags," Audrey said. "Mike is furious about Griff being left alone, and Jeff isn't far behind. I'm sure they are wondering about our relationship, and I must admit that I am wondering about it, too. Maybe in our copious free time, we could talk about that. I don't know what you're thinking, and I'm quite confused about my own thoughts these days. As Griff often says, *fish or cut bait*."

Logan nodded and said, "Yes, we should, not the *cut bait* part, but the *where do we go from here* part. I sort of made up the part about a trip to Mount St. Helens and am in favor of staying home tomorrow. We have a few things to round up here, like checking out your car and finding some new clothes, although my daughters' clothes fit you nicely. I doubt they will ever wear them again, so you are welcome to anything you want."

"That's your idea, but they might have different thoughts," Audrey said, pulling at the sleeve of the sweater she had borrowed. "I'll go shopping tomorrow, but I do kinda like this blue sweater."

"It's yours, she'll never miss it. And we need to figure out your car situation and talk to the police and insurance again about the suitcases and ski stuff we bought that Buster stole. We have a lot to do," he continued. "We can go to Mount St. Helens another time."

"Will we have another time?" Audrey asked.

"Oh, my God, yes," Logan said, moving to sit next to her. "How about all the time, Audrey? Shall I remind you again that I'm in love with you and want to be with you all the time. I could say the M-word, but I don't want to scare you off. Our society has some hard and fast rules about bigamy, and we have a lot of hurdles to leap over. Griff, Jeff, Mike, my daughters, Jan and Laura Lee, grandchildren, and neighbors."

"I am fond of you, Logan, but…"

"I know, *Griff*," Logan interrupted. "You made a vow, and the *until death do us part* phrase rings loudly in your ears, which are lovely by the way, and it would be a great honor to spend some uninterrupted time on them," he leaned over and nuzzled her lobe. "But, let's get serious, can we stop talking and do a test run on my brand new bed sheets? They have never been slept on, and I want to be sure that they work. You often toss out a list of *what ifs* and here's one for you, what if the sheets don't work. I mean, my new, super luxurious sheets could be defective and I would have to find new ones. We should test them out, just to be sure." He sighed and began again, "I love your toes, too, accosting your perfect toes as well as your ears, and I would like to accost the hell out of both your ears and your toes, as well as everything in between."

Audrey laughed, "Defective sheets, Logan? They look fine to me, but can't you see? I can't test out your sheets until I have decided: Griff or you. I love both of you in different ways and need to sort it out. It would be unfair for both you or Griff if I made a rash decision. Can we wait?"

Her now charged flip phone rang, and she looked at the number but didn't recognize it, although it was an Oregon area code. She started to answer it, but Logan pulled it away. "Don't answer it, it's probably a robocall. They call at the most inopportune times. I'm about to talk you into a bedtime story and some person is on the other end, wanting your attention as well." He closed the phone and handed it back to her.

The phone rang again, same number. This time she opened the phone and answered it. A tiny voice on the other end said, "Grandma? Can I go with you to Mount St. Helens tomorrow? Mommy said it's okay with her."

"Oh, Sophie, darling, we've decided not to go because I have so many things to do, but I'll be at your house Friday morning early when your parents are all going different directions, and we'll have a good time. We'll go to the park and zoo and wherever you want to go."

"Our parents aren't going in different directions. They're all going to Hunter to see Grandpa," the youngest, Sophie, shared with Audrey.

CHAPTER 43
Audrey

Logan laughed when Audrey told him what her granddaughter had said. "Kids always tell the truth," he said.

"It's not funny, and I'm in trouble. With Griff, with the boys and their wives, what am I going to do?" She was on the verge of tears, exhausted and disconnected from herself. "I'm throwing away my family."

Logan breathed deeply, turned toward Audrey, and slid off the couch to his knees. He winced as he set his knee to the floor, "Maybe it's time for a new family. I have an idea if you'll do it. You or I can call the boys and tell them the truth, that we are crazy about each other and you are going to leave their dad and marry me. Yes, I'm asking you to marry me because I want to spend the rest of my life with you. That's what I want, and I think you do, too. But you will have to be brave because you'll need to deal with Griff and your kids. The other option, it seems to me, is to go on living this lie, making both of us miserable and believe me, I will be miserable if you choose to return to Griff. And you will be miserable, too, Audrey." He breathed in again and clutched her hand, "Will you marry me?" Audrey was stunned. Did he know what he was saying? Marry him? She was already married, but Logan didn't seem to care. He saw the choice as clean cut, simple. Black, white, no gray, while Audrey saw only gray.

"Marry you? That would mean that I cut bait with Griff and leave him. Divorce? I don't know if I can do that. He's been my husband for nearly half a century, and I said *till death do us part*, and he's not dead yet."

Logan countered, "Audrey, forty odd years ago you made a good decision to marry Griff, but if you made the same decision today, would you choose Griff? I don't think you would. When you're in a relationship, the hope is that you grow together, but sometimes people grow apart, and that's what's happened to you and Griff. You grew together for a long time, but suddenly he became old, and well, you somehow became younger, added steam to your engine, and now you are steaming up mine."

"You are right, Logan, we have grown apart, and I'm not sure we are on a path to grow back together, but a promise is a promise. How do I decide? What if I make a bad decision?" She hadn't really thought that being with Logan would mean marrying him, in fact, this whole conversation was surreal. She couldn't leave Griff because who would take care of him?

"I learned a long time ago that the only bad decision is no decision," Logan said, firmly, attempting to rise, releasing a little grunt, "Umph. And it was a bad decision to kneel down on my knees and now I can't stand up. I'm going to have to reconsider a knee replacement. Please say yes so I don't have kneel again."

CHAPTER 44
Audrey

Logan and Audrey had been in close quarters for three days and she told Logan that she needed *thinking room* and created a cocoon on the couch to consider her dilemma. When a problem arose, she did her best thinking with a blanket, pillow, and a glass of wine, and despite being a little stiff from the drive, she curled up in a ball and sank into a daze, thinking of nothing, yet thinking about everything. Logan kissed her on her forehead and left the room, and she heard the front door open, close, and she was alone.

Sorting time, she thought as her mind ran wild and free. Is it time for common sense or serendipity? Logan had asked her to marry him, and she didn't answer. She didn't say *yes*, but she didn't say *no* either. Stay with Griff or take a chance on Logan? The devil she knew or the angel she didn't. She smiled at that one. For all she knew, Logan was a devil, too, and Griff could be an angel. Sometimes. Sex or love? Money? No, money didn't enter into this. She and Griff had enough money and she thought Logan did, as well.

She focused on Griff and all their good times, the boys, their wives, their grandchildren, whom she coined monkeys. Her mind drifted across the cows, dogs, and chickens that she had loved and the home they made far from town so many years ago. They'd had occasional trips, mostly fishing, but traveling, even fishing trips, offered her time to herself, doing what she liked, reading, hiking, or daydreaming about life beyond Hunter. She had dreamed of living in France, but it had never materialized. The cruise to Lisbon had been a blast, but would it have been as enjoyable had she not met Logan? That was the question of the week.

She thought about the bad times, mostly occurring since retirement, oddly enough. Griff was obsessed with sex and three-a-days, aspiring to have the sex drive and ability of someone who was twenty again. His constant worrying about his health and now the bunion, broken foot, sprained knee, and wrenched back. And what if he had gout or glaucoma? She doubted he would ever really be the same, yet the thought of leaving him was scary. She was a nurse, and nurses cared for people. Here she was, off with Logan, abandoning poor Griff when he most needed help.

Logan had been in constant seduction mode since she met him, dazzling her with kind acts and words, but always the gentlemen. Audrey had no doubt that he was interested in pursuing her but the words *vows*, *marriage*, and *Griff* always got in the way. When she said or indicated *go no farther*, he always backed off, but she had been close to succumbing more than once and, in fact, was thinking that she might be interested in bone jumping, after all, but seconds later, she would second-guess herself, and those long ago vows crept up inside her and permeated her soul, and she would retreat. She used to love Griff with all her heart, but now was less tolerant, especially as his mood had soured in recent years. And, as for Logan, she wasn't sure if she were in love or in deep like. Her lower forty squirmed whenever she thought of him, and anticipating having sex with him made her want it even more but didn't want to admit it to Logan as he might pressure her for more intimacy. She didn't want Griff to know, but now Griff would know because her sons were headed to Hunter and it was bulls-eye clear that Logan would be the main topic of conversation.

Her mind trailed to her mother's discussion about *enough*. Her mother had encouraged her to keep the word *enough* in her vocabulary, because she wanted Audrey to have *enough* of everything to survive on her own. *Enough* education, *enough* money, *enough* common sense. If she had those things, she could survive anything, her mother said. But now, she was thinking of the word *enough* in a different context. Had she had *enough* of Griff? Or *enough* of Logan? She couldn't have both of them, it would be far too complicated. Logan had asked her to marry him, but that meant divorcing Griff. Divorce would be complicated. They had kids, property, his health, and her apparent confusion. Maybe her kids would institutionalize her in some sort of mental health facility, treatment for her muddled mind.

"I can think of only one way to solve this," she said to herself, closed her eyes, and went to sleep.

CHAPTER 45
Logan

Logan had been alone for four years. He retired from his podiatry practice two years after Joan died, traveled two years with the goal of visiting every state capital, before he began cruising. He had managed to set foot in every state, but routing through the capitals had been tricky, and he had missed a few. His daughters lived in New York City and were glad to see him, but they kept busy with their own lives, which didn't include him, and he left after only a few days. Traveling by car meant he saw a lot of the country, but he also had to pack and unpack, find a community laundromat every week or so, and take a chance with restaurants whose appearances deceived the quality of the food. And he was alone.

During his travels, he had met a lot of women, but none appealed to him, and he walked away, time after time. Some women continued their pursuit, but he always gently turned them away. Until he met Audrey.

He found Audrey physically attractive, like many women, but he was blindsided by the overwhelming and unstoppable sexual emotions that emerged the first time he set eyes on her. At first, he wondered if she had performed some sort of magic on him, cast a spell, but as he came to know her better, it was her innocence, her honesty, her vitality, and he later admitted, her perfect toes that had seduced him.

She and Griff had been married a long time, and she looked at their marriage as a corked bottle of fine wine, preserved forever, not to be opened. Logan had thought that way, too, until he lost Joan and his thinking shifted. He had loved Joan, but he was in love with Audrey and it was not the same thing. When he met Audrey, he was swept off his feet, totally smitten, and could hardly look at her without his libido coming to life. In his mind, although they had only recently met, they were one, one soul, one being. Being her kindred spirit was a new concept, but it filled him as nothing ever had before. Trying to make sense of his emotions, he pondered the difference between love and sex, but when Audrey came into view, any differences evaporated. With Audrey, sex and love, and even their separate beings, were indistinguishable. He was seventy years old and knew that life was too short to disregard these cravings, awkward or not. Being alone was no fun nor was being lonely. He wanted Audrey and didn't want to share her with Griff or anyone else.

The question that echoed in his head was how. He had asked her to marry him, but she hadn't answered, which he considered a no. How could he convince Audrey to spend the rest of her life with him? They were so alike, yet so different, and he knew she was frightened. She would be leaving a relationship that she had fostered most of her life to step into something new and unknown. No wonder she was scared. Joan had been gone four years and he had rejected all the women who had pursued him. Why should he expect Audrey not to do the same to him?

Logan felt afraid, too, afraid she would accept his marriage proposal, which would mean entering uncharted waters that held sharks and piranha, possibly named Jeff, Mike, Jan, or Laura Lee. He also feared that she would say no, and he would be alone again, and he would never find another Audrey.

CHAPTER 46
Audrey

Audrey showed up at Mike and Abby's house right on time saying, "I can't wait to spoil you, my little monkeys! I'm going to give you grandma love all week." Mike and Abby's two daughters sat at the kitchen table in their pajamas eating pancakes. "I brought donuts from the bakery but save some for your cousins." She passed them the box, and they each grabbed two. Mike and Abby had two girls, Sophie aged eight and Emma aged ten. Jeff and his family had not yet arrived.

They were all her monkeys, but they were growing up too fast. Emma was already taller than Audrey and wore the same size shoe. Sophie was up to her shoulder, but she spent most of her time up-side-down, standing on her head, so it was actually her feet that reached Audrey's shoulder.

Mike handed Audrey a cup of coffee and steered her into the living room, "Where's your friend?" he asked with a smirk. "Isn't he coming, too?"

"If you mean Logan, he has his own plans for today, so no, he's not coming. I am not sure exactly what's on his agenda," she fibbed, knowing his agenda included her, but she would keep that a secret.

"How was the drive to Mount St. Helens? He said you'd never seen it, but we went the last time you were here, don't you remember?" Mike knew that Logan and Audrey had stayed in Portland but probed for an answer anyway.

"We didn't go. I had to do some shopping, and the car was yucky from the rain and muddy roads and needed a bath, and I needed to rest. I fell asleep early and slept late, and we decided to stay home and rest," Audrey explained, truthfully. She had fallen asleep on Logan's couch and hadn't rallied until morning.

"Mom, are you sleeping with him? I might as well ask you because it's something we all want to know," Mike blurted out. "Why didn't you tell us about Dad? You know that you didn't have to come; we could have found someone else to stay with the kids. You know that. You have first right of refusal but no obligation." Mike raised his voice, and a moment later Abby entered the room. "You should be home with Dad, not running around the country with some foot doctor."

"Mike, settle down, for Pete's sake. Personally, Audrey, I hope you are sleeping with him. Griff has become a little strange in the past couple years, and I think a fling with the foot doctor would be a good thing," Abby said, beaming at both of them. "You deserve some happiness, and if Dr. Logan makes you happy, go for it. He's handsome and funny and I like him, and he obviously is fond of you. It's sweet."

"Sweet? Harrumph. That's the trouble," Mike said. "She's already married, and she didn't answer my question."

"What question?" Abby interjected.

"Is everybody ready to go?" Jeff called as he and Lizzy and their kids stormed through the door. "Let's get this show on the road. Hi, Mom, are you ready for a fun time with the wild bunch?" Jeff's two kids spied the donuts and emptied the box.

Audrey caught up with her sons and wives just as they were exiting the house, "Tell your dad hello. Tell him I'll be back home as soon as you guys return to Huckleberry. Don't worry about a thing."

Mike and Jeff stopped to stare at Audrey, and shrugged, as if to say, how did she know? "Be good for Grandma," the parents called to their children as they exited the house and got into the car.

Oh, Lord, now what do I do?

CHAPTER 47
Griff

With Audrey out of town, the house was quiet. Griff had no one to talk to and settled in to watching some of his favorite shows on the sex channels, which ran most of the day. He watched two days straight, breaking only for beer, meals, and an occasional bathroom trip. Some of the actresses were really hot, but Audrey wasn't here, and he didn't like to diddle himself, so he finally began looking for other diversions. He didn't want to read books or magazines so quickly returned to television. He tried a few old movies on a classics channel and westerns on the western channel but became bored with Marshall Dillon and Chester and flipped back to SXTV.

Steve dropped by late on the fourth day and the two of them broke out a six-pack. Steve pulled a frozen pizza from the freezer and popped it in the oven to cook. "Why is Audrey with Logan?" Steve asked. "Did they plan this, or did it just happen? Carlee thought he had his eye on her on our trip, but she sometimes exaggerates."

"I don't know, Audrey said that he went with her because he needed a ride to Portland, but he's a sneaky devil, and I'm guessing he planned it," Griff said, shaking his head. "He has his eye on her, that's for sure, which upsets me, but she denies it. He hovers around her like a swarm of bees. I don't know what's happened to her because she seems to have a screw loose about a lot of things since she went into menopause."

Steve agreed, "You are right, brother, only, it isn't just Audrey, it's all women. They lose it when they reach their peaks, they think their marital warranty is up. I traded my first wife in on Carlee, I considered her the answer to my prayers, a trophy wife, because she was really hot, but now that she's sixty, although still hot, she's lapsing into some of the same strange habits that my ex did. It's like she's tossing me aside and doesn't care about me. Through the years I've learned that women prefer romance to sex, and she's fallen into that trap. She doesn't seem to enjoy *doing it* anymore, claiming she's too tired or too busy or too sore or has to go shopping or something. Lame excuses. But I don't have the energy to trade her in now that her warranty is expiring. Courting a new wife is a lot of work."

She wasn't too tired for me; it was like the triple crown of sheet dancing. That girl wore me out, Griff remembered. He did not like Carlee's excessive use of alcohol but appreciated her eagerness to explore new ways to satisfy him. She had stirred him in ways Audrey never had. "I'm not looking for a new wife either," Griff said, "I like the one I have, and a double benefit, she's a nurse and can take care of me. I don't want a new model. She's fine, but I have to figure out this Logan thing. She never talks about him but is ready as Portland cement to go with him or call him or have him for a meal. I can't help but wonder why she's off with him while I'm trapped in the house. I don't understand why she likes him, she's always been happy, especially since we do our three-a-days. Since she met him, she's been cranky, and I would like to have the old Audrey back."

Steve was thinking of Phyllis who filled his void whenever she came near. "Women are hard to figure out, that's for sure, and they become real puzzles when they go through the change. Do you have anything going on the side? I mean, are you poking around with anyone else, some other lovely fish in the sea. Watch the papers, men die, women don't."

"Not really, I mean, I saw a couple hotties on the cruise, and even spent some quality time with a couple, but nothing here," Griff pointed to his cast and said, "I'm housebound right now, although Audrey is gone. If I didn't have this confounded cast, it might be a perfect time for a little canoodling."

CHAPTER 48
Griff

It was Phyllis' day to check in with Griff, and she came in with a box filled with sweet things to eat that she had picked up at the bakery. When she arrived at Griff and Audrey's house, he was asleep on the couch. He didn't answer the door, but she went in anyway, and he was softly snoring. He was wearing shorts and had propped up his feet on pillows with a cast on his right leg, and his left ankle wrapped with an elastic bandage, and the bunion splint for his big toe. His white t-shirt contained dribbles of something brown, he hadn't shaved for several days, and needed a haircut. The TV was running, some girls having sex with each other, and she turned it off before he opened his eyes and saw it. She was sure that SXTV had been flipped on by accident.

"Griff, Griff, wake up. It's Phyllis, I'm just checking in."

Griff opened his eyes, yawned, and pulled himself into a sitting position. "Oh, Phyllis. Thanks for coming by. I'm glad to see you. How are you doing? How's Gus?" His hair was pointed in several directions, and he tried to comb it with his fingers.

"Gus is better, not home yet, but better. I'll make some coffee, and I brought you a few cookies. Snickerdoodles, my favorites," she said. "Have you heard from Audrey? How is her babysitting gig going? She was crazy to see her little monkey-kins, as she calls them."

"I don't know because she hasn't called. She's supposed to take care of me and now she has deserted me," Griff complained.

Phyllis retorted, "Well, can't you call her? Don't you have her cell number?"

"Sure, I have it, but she said she would call, and she hasn't," Griff countered. "It's her duty to call me. She's paying more attention to that foot quack and doesn't seem to care about me any longer."

"She's probably busy with the grandchildren. She was looking forward to some outings, like the zoo, the park, and even some shopping. Knowing Audrey, she'll probably set the kids up with a reading schedule and make a few trips to the library, too," Phyllis laughed.

"She's busy, all right, with that quack, Logan, that's the problem," Griff grumbled. "He is definitely a problem."

Phyllis had suspected that Audrey and Logan had a *thing* but was mystified as to why Griff couldn't solve the problem. "So, Griff, why is he the problem? You and Audrey have been married a long time. He's a nice man, but she would not choose him over you unless she had an issue. Have you done something that has made her look at someone else? It seems to me that if you love her, you'll give her room to grow and make sure she knows you love her as well. If her job is to take care of you, your job is to take care of her. Are you taking care of her? She loves you, so don't borrow trouble. Don't overreact and give her a reason to go with Logan. It sounds like you are taking her for granted."

Griff said, "Phyllis, I want to ask you two questions. What's more important to women? Sex or romance? And exactly what is romance?"

"Why are you asking?"

"Steve was here yesterday, and said that women like romance more than sex, but I can hardly believe that. What woman would be crazy enough not to love *doing the dirty* multiple times a day?"

"I'll answer your questions, but first let's talk about your term *doing the dirty*. How about eliminating the term *doing the dirty* and replacing it with something romantic?"

"Like what," Griff chortled, "bumping bellies?"

"No, like *making love* or *Audrey time at its best* or *building a love nest*, something that focuses on Audrey and her needs, not the actual sex act," she explained.

Griff lit up like he had an idea, "How about *hot beef syringe*?" he teased, immediately adding, "I know, I'm just teasing, don't get all huffy. Audrey told me once that she didn't like that term, and I disposed of it a long time ago."

"Ix-nay to both of those, you need to find a new term. *Doing the dirty*, well, it's not exactly an inviting term," Phyllis said bluntly.

"What then? Audrey likes it, at least she's never said she didn't," Griff argued.

"I'm sure we can think of something. And as for sex versus romance, they are both important, but women want them combined. I mean like, when you and I did the horizontal hula on the ship, we had danced and cuddled a little before. You nibbled on my ear, which I found sexy as hell. Gus' term, *doing the horizontal hula*, struck me as funny, not grubby like *doing the dirty*. Gus and I cuddle and tease each other with words and sexual actions, and it's that foreplay that turns me on. I love sex, but not without stimulation. After Gus figured that out, we have had a great sex life. When he gained all that weight, we continued to fondle each other and pleased each other in a lot of ways. What I'm saying is that romance is mandatory if you want a relationship to thrive."

Phyllis paused before continuing, "Men often assume that women enjoy the same things as they do and have the same needs but generally speaking, women want romance while men want sex, plain and simple, and although the two are compatible, both sexes have to give and sometimes give a lot. In my mind, romance is all about giving and sex is taking. Sex is not more important than romance, and romance is not more important than sex. Some men are hell-bent to have sex on demand, and it wears women out. I want sex, but Gus eases into sex through his romantic moves, making me one happy woman."

"I don't see a difference," Griff retorted. "Sex is what marriage is about, not silly romance stuff."

Phyllis answered, "Hold it a minute, mister, do you think that the romance stuff is silly? I don't, and I'm sure Audrey doesn't either. No woman does."

"What romance stuff are you talking about? Griff grunted, "Dinner and a movie? We go to the movies once in a while, when Stallone makes a new film. She likes those stupid romantic comedies, but I hate them, and if I'm paying three bucks for a movie, I want action. I like action."

Phyllis laughed as she continued, "Three bucks for a movie? When was the last time you invited her to a movie? They cost about eight or ten dollars per person these days, except for the third-run dollar shows. Does she love the Stallone movies? I doubt it."

"She has never said, but they are great movies, and Stallone is a great actor," Griff answered. "The last movie we saw in a theater was *Raiders of the Lost Ark*. Our kids went with us, and went out for pizza after. Now that was a great movie."

Phyllis was shocked. "Yes, Griff, *Raiders of the Lost Ark* was a great movie, but it came out in about the eighties. Is that the last time you took her to a movie?"

"Gas is expensive just to go all the way into town for a movie, Griff complained. "*Raiders* might have been our last movie in a theater, but we have Prime, which is free. It's cheaper to watch it here, and we don't have to drive all the way to town to see something."

Phyllis continued, "Going to the movies is a great way to romance and flirt and you should give in to the romantic comedies. You could actually turn the tables and suggest a romantic comedy. It would be spontaneous, and she would love it. You won't die, and maybe you'll learn something about Audrey. Besides movies, she might want to try sexy delights, like roses or chocolate, or fun surprises, you know, something spontaneous like breakfast in bed or a picnic that you plan and prepare for her? Women eat up that kind of thing."

"The cruise was spontaneous, and besides that, it cost a ton of money and we didn't go on the cheap. I just picked this cruise, and we went. Spontaneously," Griff responded. "She fixes breakfast, so I don't how she could have breakfast in bed. You're talking crazy."

"That's what I'm talking about. YOU picked the cruise. Did Audrey have a choice? Did you ask her where she wanted to go? I'm sure she would have picked France if she had her choice. And why don't you fix her breakfast some morning? She's probably fixed you breakfast nearly every day since you've been married, so switch it out a bit. Surprise her. Gus fixes me breakfast every Sunday, but in the summer, he would make it into a patio breakfast picnic."

"No, I didn't ask her which cruise because Steve and Gus had already set their itinerary, and it left the next day. She had never met Steve and Gus, but obviously they're great guys. She tried to take me to France one year, but we went fishing instead. Lisbon can't be much different than Paris," Griff argued.

"Are you kidding, Griff? Lisbon and Paris are vastly different," Phyllis paused, puzzled at his bullheadedness. "Continuing my plea for romance, when was the last time you rubbed her feet? Or wrote her a poem or love note? Or put candles on the table?"

"Poem? Oh, for heck's sake, I can't write a poem, I'm a farmer. And the last time we used candles, she put them in the bathroom, and look what happened, a broken foot and a head injury. I'm the one with foot troubles, she should be rubbing my feet," Griff said bluntly.

Phyllis smiled, "Don't you like a little foreplay, Griff, I mean like when she tickles your ears and other parts of your body, or rubs your feet, or just snuggles up to you? I dig the softer romantic stuff, all lovey dovey, warm and fuzzy. Poems definitely turn women on, including me, or maybe especially me. And gentle, meaningful caresses go a long way toward good sex."

"So, you're insisting that this romance stuff is a must?" Griff queried. "It seems like a lot of bother to me."

"Yup, clearly. Are you and Audrey having trouble between the sheets?" Phyllis was thinking that something else was going on.

Griff guffawed, "No, of course not, but when she comes back from her babysitting duties, and my foot heals, and my bunion disappears and my back stops aching, we'll want to have some bedroom fun. But it sounds like I have to do some romance, right? I don't even know what that is. What should I do?"

Phyllis started laughing, "I could give you the dictionary definition if you like, but examples might be better. It would probably surprise you to know that Gus is a romantic guy, and when we both worked, he left love notes in my lunch bag regularly, sometimes a poem or quote from an author I liked, or a hand drawn heart. Simple. Didn't cost anything, and I kept most of them. He tried writing poetry, but wasn't particularly good at it, but it came as a surprise and brightened my day. One time he wrote, *Roses are red, and I love Phyllis, almost as much as I love Dobie Gillis.* It was a bad poem, but I laughed when I read it, and I knew he had done his best.

"When we first married, every time we argued or one of us had a bad day, he would bring me a banana split. After a dozen years, it broke my heart to tell him I hate banana splits, but he sprang into action and began bringing hot fudge sundaes, which I do love.

"Every Valentine's Day, he would buy funny Valentine's shorts and parade through the house, declaring his love for me. Our first year of marriage, it was strange, but through the years, it became funnier and now I have a whole drawer of Valentine's Day shorts. Best of all, he nibbles my ears and neck, which turns my sexual gears to overdrive." Phyllis giggled at the thought of Gus parading through the house in his hot Valentine's Day shorts.

CHAPTER 49
Carlee

By any standard, Carlee looked hot when she arrived to check on Griff on Friday afternoon. She wore silver cropped leggings with a magenta spaghetti-strapped, open-shoulder top with loose sleeves to cover her sun-wrinkled arms. She wore sandals and carried a wide-brimmed hat and matching handbag and looked like she had stepped out of a fashion magazine. Her flawless make-up covered her face, reducing, but not eliminating, her ever-present face creases.

Griff tried to stand when she entered the house. He knew Audrey had set today as Carlee's day to check on him and had been looking forward to her visit. As he lifted himself from the sofa, gravity and unsteadiness plopped him down. He combined his greeting and his plopping to "Carlumph," and waited. She didn't disappoint, and, in a heartbeat, she was next to him, kissing him, and he was kissing her back, "Oh, Carlee, I'm glad to see you. It's been a long time, and I've missed you."

Griff had been mulling over Phyllis' comment about sex versus romance. She seemed to think that romance was the key to keeping Audrey, but it was a foreign idea, and he would need to practice. He had devised several romantic scenarios and thought if he could try a couple, he might be able to woo Audrey away from the quack. Carlee was just the person to practice on.

Phyllis had made a point about using poetry, so he had written a poem to Carlee for practice. He would pen a poem expressing his love for Audrey before she came home next week, plenty of time to write a really good one. His first attempt was: *To Carlee, Roses are red, and Carlee is purty, how about it, my dear, shall we do the dirty?* But then, he remembered he should not use the words *do the dirty* and wadded it up and threw it in the trash. Second try, he thought it was better. *To Carlee, I adore you, Carlee, it's no joke, let's not waste time, let's go for a poke.* He and Audrey had seen *Lonesome Dove* on television, and he remembered that the Robert Duvall, playing Gus, had used the term *poke*.

It was his first attempt at poetry since high school, so he knew it was rough, and maybe Carlee wasn't like other women, but he'd give it a whirl. "Carlee, I'm trying to become more romantic and began writing poetry. Today I wrote a poem for you. It's my first and it's short, but I hope you like it." He read it aloud to her, and she stared at him with an open mouth, dumbfounded. It was pure Griff, coarse and to the point.

"Oh, Griff, it's a...little direct...but no one has ever written a poem for me. Not Steve, not my ex, not my kids. Oh, Griff, I'm...speechless." She had been hoping Griff would be interested in some sheet-rolling and pressed up against him, whispering, "You've set my body on fire. Do you think we could do the dirty?"

Thinking quickly, Griff said, "Oh, Honey, I don't want to do the dirty, that's coarse and grimy, but I would like to play some games in Carlee's love nest."

A happy tear dropped from Carlee's eye as she helped him into the wheelchair and aimed him to the bedroom where they could extinguish her fire.

Griff smiled to himself, *Griff, you devil dog, you're such a fast learner.*

CHAPTER 50
Griff

The drive from Huckleberry had been an easy one, hardly any traffic, and Mike's new SUV had a radar detector. Since he could boost his speed to eighty or higher, they arrived earlier than they normally would have. They had not called Griff because he seldom answered the phone anyway, and he was home with a broken foot, so where could he possibly go? He'd be home, they were sure. When they arrived at the house, a navy blue Volvo sat in the driveway. It looked new but was covered with a light layer of dust. "Did Dad find new wheels?" Mike asked. "If so, Mom doesn't know about it, as she talked about his old pick-up. Our parents are kicking out some musty cobwebs."

"Dad? Dad, are you home?" Jeff hollered as he opened the front door. "Dad, it's us, Mike and Jeff. Lizzy and Abby, too. Are you home? Where are you?"

"Oh, crap," Griff hissed to Carlee, "where'd they come from? They said they were going fishing at Tahoe. You have to hide. Go in the bathroom."

Carlee leapt out of bed and scurried into the bathroom, covering herself with one of Audrey's robes. She grabbed her clothes from the floor, forgetting her sandals, and hid behind the shower curtain to redress.

Griff called as loudly as he could, "I'm in the bathroom cleaning up. I didn't know you were coming. I'll be out in a minute. Audrey said you were going to Tahoe." The last thing he wanted was their coming into his bedroom.

"We changed our mind. The fishing in Hunter is good, and we can kill two birds with one stone, fish and see you. And we don't have to pay for a hotel room," Mike called back to him.

Although the weather remained cold and it had been raining all day, his jeans didn't fit over his cast, so Griff threw on a clean pair of shorts and polo shirt. He attached a sandal to his left foot and sat down in the wheelchair to roll himself out to the kitchen where his family waited for him to make an appearance.

"That's a pretty fancy ride in the driveway, Dad. It beats the old pickup to heck and back. Mom didn't tell us you bought a new one. You two are spending money like crazy. A cruise and now new wheels. I'm impressed," said Jeff.

"That car? Oh, it's not mine," Griff replied. His mind was racing. *How in the heck can Carlee leave our house, and what did I do with the poem?* "Where are your suitcases? Why don't you bring them into the house? You can sleep in your old rooms," Griff said.

Carlee was having the exact same thoughts as Griff, but she had forgotten about the poem. How would she get out of the house and go home without Griff's family seeing her? *I'm in trouble*, she thought to herself. She had dressed herself and was sitting on the edge of the bathtub, trying to plan something, anything.

The four went outside while Griff bee-lined it to his bedroom as fast as he could in his wheelchair. He found one of Audrey's old nursing uniforms in the closet and handed it to Carlee. "Carlee, put this on because you're going to be my nurse today. I'm going to tell them you come every day to help me." He held her face and kissed her and said, "Trust me, Carlee, it's a great idea."

Carlee nodded and started to put it on. Audrey was five foot nothing and Carlee was nearly six feet tall, but they wore the same size dresses. Audrey's nursing uniform had sat below her knees, but on Carlee, it rode high, encroaching on her derrière. She pulled on the silver leggings and looked at herself in the mirror. *Black would have been better, but this will have to do*, she thought.

"Where's the poem?" Griff asked.

"What poem?" she returned.

"You know, the one I wrote to you, about having a poke."

"Oh, I forgot about that one. I don't know. I don't have it, so it must be by the couch," she answered.

"Well, find it," Griff ordered. "I've gotta pee."

CHAPTER 51
Griff

Carlee peeked around the corner before she tiptoed into the living room, hoping not to see his family. She didn't. She moved toward the couch to search for the damaging sheet of paper he had written his Carlee poem on, positive that he hadn't given it to her. With Audrey away, the house was a cluttered mess. There were cans and papers and a few dishes with food remnants on them, but she did not see the poem. She heard the kitchen door slam, followed by people chattering and laughing, and then suddenly the house was filled with silence. Dead silence. She turned around to face four people who she had never seen before.

"Who are you?" one of the men asked.

She tugged at the hem of Audrey's uniform, trying to lengthen it, "Uh, uh, I'm a nurse. I'm here to help your dad. I'm just tidying up. My name's Carlee. He's better than when he first came home."

Lizzy whispered to Jeff, "Your mom was a nurse, but she wore her dresses down to her knees. Is that your mom's dress? It looks like the one we gave her for Christmas a few years ago. Remember? It had those little red roses embroidered on the collar."

Jeff nodded, "Things have changed. Nobody dresses like Mom anymore, not even Mom." He remembered the blue cashmere sweater she wore at the Vertigo restaurant. With its low-cut neckline, it was not a mom-type sweater.

"We didn't know he had a nurse because neither he nor our mom told us. Is that your car, Carlee? It's pretty nice," Mike said. "Nurses must make a lot of money these days."

"Yes, it is, and I was just about to go home. I only stay for an hour or two. Depending," Carlee said. "I just need to put my shoes on, and I'll get out of your hair."

Mike, the suspicious one, asked, "Depending on what?"

"Why, depending on what he needs, of course. Today, he needed a rub down, you know, his back."

Griff came out of the bedroom, and said, "I see that you've met my nurse. She was just about to leave, aren't you? Did you find that piece of paper I lost?"

"No, sir, I didn't; do you want me to keep looking?"

"Look a little bit more, it has to be here somewhere," Griff said. "You guys take your suitcases upstairs. We don't need your help." All he needed was for one of his kids to find that paper and he would be toast. It was a mistake to have listened to Phyllis. What did she know?

CHAPTER 52
Griff

Nobody wanted to cook after their long drive, so Griff suggested they call their nearest neighbor Rosemary Sage to see what she had available. She catered events but could be counted on for a variety of pastas and sauces and most likely would have salad makings and possibly some freshly baked bread. She was delighted to receive their call and was happy to accommodate Audrey's family. She was a wonderful cook, and they couldn't wait to test her wares. Mike and Jeff headed to pick up the food while Abby and Lizzy stayed behind to declutter, with Lizzy tending to the kitchen while Abby attacked the living room.

Griff and Carlee had not yet found his Carlee poem. With Carlee gone and Abby in cleaning mode, Griff was in a panic. He didn't trust Abby, who no doubt would report the poem to Mike, who would blab to Audrey. No telling what Audrey would do. Lizzy could be more reasonable and might even laugh about Griff's poem.

Lizzy began rinsing dishes and wiping down counters and the table. "Griff, don't you ever wash dishes? This stuff is caked on, and I'm gonna have to hand wash them before I put them in the dishwasher."

"Phyllis washed some dishes when she was here yesterday."

"Who's Phyllis?" Abby asked. Did Griff have a stream of women coming in to see him?

"Phyllis Gustafson, she went on the cruise with us. Her husband, Gus, is in the hospital, and Audrey asked Phyllis to stop by to check on me. She was a schoolteacher when Mike and Jeff went to high school," Griff told her.

"How about your sexy nurse? I would think she would be able to help a bit," Abby suggested as she sorted through piles of newspapers, mail, and other clutter.

"She's a nurse, not a maid," Griff answered tersely. He definitely could not ask Carlee to wash his dishes. She could do lots of things, but not that.

"What's with the kitchen sink, Griff? It isn't draining," Lizzy called from the kitchen.

"Audrey's been complaining about it, but I can't fix it until I heal all these confounded injuries. She wanted to hire a plumber, but they're too expensive, so I told her to wait. It drains, but it's slow."

"It's unusable as it is, so we have to do something. I'll ask Jeff and Mike to take a look. Between the two of them, they should be able to clear it. The trap might need to be flushed out. It shouldn't take long, and they can do it after dinner tonight or tomorrow before they go fishing," Lizzy offered.

He was growing more and more upset that he could not find the poem. If he made a fuss, they would want to know exactly what he had lost. Maybe he had left it in the bedroom. "Gotta pee," he announced, as he wheeled himself into the bedroom.

The bedroom was just as they had left it, chaotic. The bed was unmade with clothes strewn around. Carlee had taken her handbag, but her matching sunhat sat on the floor and the magenta shirt was on the bathroom floor. He threw them in the bathtub and closed the shower curtain. Griff saw his other clothes lying on the floor and remembered that he had changed clothes when the boys arrived. He found Carlee's poem deep in the hip pocket of his dirty clothes. He folded it up, creasing the corners, and tossed it in the wastebasket.

All was well.

CHAPTER 53
Griff

Rosemary created a feast of chicken enchiladas, salad, freshly baked bread, and chocolate chip cookies. And she threw in a few bottles of wine to boot. This was welcome help since Hunter lay over half an hour's drive from their farm, so going to a restaurant was not on the agenda, especially with Griff's injuries. Rain had drizzled much of the day, and the temperature dropped, icing over the roads and sidewalks. They enjoyed their meal and emptied two and a half bottles of wine among the five of them.

"Let's fix the drain tonight so we can fish all day tomorrow, assuming this rain goes away. The drain probably needs to be flushed. There's usually a drain snake in the shop, I'll go find it," Mike said.

"Bring a pipe wrench, too," Jeff reminded. "The screw on the trap is bound to be stuck."

"I can do this, help me to the floor," Griff insisted. "You guys don't need to do it. I can."

Mike said, "No, Dad, you have a broken foot and you guzzled a little wine. We can unclog it, but you rest because you might hurt yourself. You're running out of feet and legs to hurt, so just get out of the way and let us do it for you."

Mike's last comment, to *get out of the way*, outraged Griff, "No, I can do it. Everybody's treating me like a baby, like I can't do anything. I'm not drunk, and I've fixed more drains than you ever will in your lifetime. It's my danged house, my danged sink, and my danged drain. I'll do it."

Not wanting to have a verbal altercation with his father, Jeff didn't answer as he rolled Griff's wheelchair away from the front of the sink, and moments later, Mike and Jeff knelt down, trying to unscrew the trap before Griff tried to do it himself.

Griff was sulking and swearing to himself and his brow tightened and his face reddened. "I can do it, and I'm not drunk," he mumbled over and over.

After one good turn, the trap began leaking, and Lizzy supplied a large dishpan to catch the murky, stinky water, and sludge began pouring from the kitchen drain. Griff, continuing to recite his mantra, watched from his wheelchair as the water and muck spilled into the dishpan. It filled the pan, and Griff griped, "You could at least let me do that much. Hand me the pan, and I'll throw it outside."

Jeff and Mike looked at each other and shrugged, "Okay, if it will make you happy." They passed the dishpan to Griff, and he began to roll toward the back door with the filthy water sloshing onto his lap. Lizzy opened the back door, and Griff rolled himself onto the icy stoop. His hands balanced the dishpan, and he didn't set the wheelchair brake. He heaved the water to the frozen dirt, gained momentum, and crashed into the handrail, nearly tipping himself over. One wheel slid off the stoop, leaving Griff balancing precariously. Attempting to keep Griff from going over the side of stoop, Lizzy grabbed at the chair, slipped on the ice, and collapsed to her backside on the ice-covered step.

"Are you hurt, Lizzy?" Jeff called out. Jeff and Mike sprang to their feet and rushed to her side. They helped her up, brushed her off, and escorted her to the kitchen. The door slammed shut leaving Griff teetering on the step.

"Hey, what about me?" he called after them.

CHAPTER 54
Griff

Jeff and Mike arose early to head to one of the streams famous for trout. Griff had wanted to go, but they wouldn't allow it, and Lizzy and Abby stayed behind to help.

"I don't need a babysitter," Griff pleaded. "What's with you kids? I'm fine."

"I bruised my bum," Lizzy explained, "and I'm not going anywhere." She was lying on the couch with an ice pack propped under her. "I'll watch a movie or something." She turned on the TV, and SXTV channel flashed on. "Oh, my gosh, who put this on the TV?" she said aloud, immediately thinking of the nurse in the mini dress. Was that nurse person Carlee watching TV when she should have been taking care of Griff? She flashed it off and found a movie. She'd let Jeff call the nursing service because this was definitely unacceptable behavior.

Abby disappeared to do some yoga before tackling a few more household chores. The boys hadn't finished the drain trap until late and the dishwasher ran during the night. She unloaded several days' worth of dishes and refilled it with breakfast bowls and plates. When this was done, she began wandering around the house, looking for something else to do. She could have been at a yoga retreat instead of watching a drain being repaired and now, she had pent-up energy to burn.

Griff was napping on a couch and Lizzy was tuned into a movie, so Abby moved from room to room looking for something to do and settled on straightening up Audrey and Griff's bedroom. She stripped the bed and threw the sheets in the washer, hoping clean sheets would improve her father-in-law's mood. She wiped out the bathroom sink and refilled the toilet paper holder and picked up the trash, which was overflowing, mostly with tissue paper, as well as one full-sized sheet of paper, that she found folded neatly in quarters on top. She pulled it out of the basket. *To Carlee, I adore you, Carlee, it's no joke, let's not waste time, let's for a poke.*

Abby laughed aloud, *time for a poke*, what the heck? She had watched *Lonesome Dove* and knew what poke meant, but she'd never heard it used otherwise. Griff, in his crudest, used *doing the dirty* and Mike teased her with the same. Wasn't Carlee the bombshell nurse's name? Were Griff and Carlee *poking*? What the heck? Well, isn't that interesting? Old Griff bonking his nurse. Or was she a nurse? She kinda looked like a hooker, but Abby knew Griff pinched pennies and would never pay for a hooker. Did Audrey know?

She stuck the Carlee note in her hip pocket but tossed the other trash in the can and returned it to the bathroom. She peeked in the shower, wondering if it needed cleaning and hoping it didn't, and had another what-the-heck moment? An oversized hat and a size 38 blouse. A nice one with a designer label size forty that she knew wasn't Audrey's. Audrey wore a size thirty-four or thirty-six, and with Audrey's ginger colored hair, magenta would have been a no-no, and Audrey didn't wear shoulder-less blouses anyway, or at least she'd never seen her in one. She placed the blouse on a hanger and hung it in the closet.

CHAPTER 55
Jeff and Mike

Mike and Jeff remembered a fishing hole from their childhood and aimed toward it. "Dad's a mess," Jeff said. "I don't know how Mom will be able to handle him when she comes back. She's not strong like she used to be, and he's full of beans most of the time."

Mike answered, "I don't know what's going on with either of them. Have they become senile? First the cruise, with first class accommodations, and all Dad's injuries, and now Mom has a boyfriend. They've been married forever, so what's going on? And what are we going to do about it."

"We should call her, but let's wait until we are home. Maybe Dad will be in a better mood, and she's inevitably more pleasant than he is. Lizzy and Abby should have a fun day," Jeff said sarcastically.

"Oh, yeah, a day with Dad, that'll be a barrel of laughs," Mike laughed, mockingly. "Let's stop at the convenience store to buy our licenses and grab some grub and beer."

The fish had gone on strike, so after four hours, they left empty-handed, beer, sandwiches, and fish had all gone away. They could try again tomorrow.

Since they were fishless, they stopped at the grocery store and bought some steak and Idaho bakers before they headed to the house where they found Abby and Lizzy had involved themselves in a serious game of gin rummy with wine glasses in front of them. Lizzy had discovered another poem that Griff had written to Carlee, and the two had giggled about them all afternoon. Griff was perched on the front porch drinking a beer with his head tilted to the side, and it looked like he was napping.

"How'd the day go? Are you better? Is your cute little derriere healing?" Jeff asked Lizzy. "You landed pretty hard."

"Yes, it's better. Icing it helped a lot, but we each found something that you two might want to know."

"Yeah, what's that?" Mike said. "Did dear old Dad do something else that was crazy?"

Abby answered, "Crazy? Maybe. I found this note, a poem, in the bathroom, and Lizzy found another wadded up in the kitchen trash. I think this is what he was in a panic about when we arrived."

"What do you mean a poem?" Mike answered. "Dad doesn't do poetry, I guarantee it."

"I agree with you because they are not great, but let me read them to you." She read each poem aloud, exaggerating the words, and they burst into laughter as she read *do the dirty*.

Jeff agreed, "You're right, it's not much of a poem. Who's Carlee?"

"The nurse, the hot nurse with all the wrinkles, her name was Carlee," Abby said. "And, I found a designer magenta blouse and woman's sunhat in the bathtub, of all places, and I don't think they are your mom's. Maybe Carlee's, though."

Lizzy said, "I, too, have an interesting addition to the mystery. I watched movies today, and when I turned the TV on, it clicked on to SXTV. I couldn't believe it because Audrey would never consider watching it, so it must be Griff. Or Carlee. Or the pair of them."

Mike picked up the Carlee note and said, "Yup, this is Dad's handwriting. I don't know whether to be outraged, confused, saddened, or alarmed."

Jeff said, "I'm the same, I don't know what to think, but you gotta admit it's funny. I'm laughing my ass off."

"We should call Audrey," Lizzy said, "she needs to know about Griff, and I trust her to tell us the truth more than I trust him, but what about

Logan? She's not saying much about him. Do you think your mom and Logan are having a fling?"

Abby chimed in, "Audrey and Logan are cute. Who cares if they are having a fling? She deserves some happiness after being stranded, I mean being stranded eighteen miles outside of town all these years, in the middle of a fishing and hunting mecca while Griff did both, and she did neither. She never complained, and maybe she's just spreading her wings. Anyway, who's going to call your mom?"

Three fingers pointed at Jeff who poured himself a beer before dialing. He put it on speaker mode and shushed everyone.

"Mom, this is Jeff. How's it going? You're on speaker phone, but everyone's outside," he fibbed. "How are you holding up?"

"I'm fine, we are all having fun, but they sure have a lot of energy. I guess that's why God gives children to young people and not to women of a certain age, as they say." She let out a laugh, but thought, *ain't that the truth?*

"Are they too much for you?" Jeff asked, hesitantly. His father had aged rapidly, and he hoped his mother had not.

"Not really, but they keep me going. We stayed home today, playing some games, but tomorrow we will have a busy day. We are going to the park to see what's new for the younger two. The older two aren't so keen on the park but are excited to help me set up a new phone that they're going to help me choose. I'm going to buy one of those magic phones that does everything, so we will hit the phone store after the park. We will also have ice cream," Audrey explained.

Abby mouthed, *ask about Logan.*

Jeff complied, "How about Logan, Mom, have you seen him this week? Is he helping you?"

"We've talked by phone a couple times, and he's going to meet us in the park, add his two cents' worth about the phone, and join us for ice cream. He doesn't have any grandchildren, so he'll probably learn some things. How's your dad? Is he having pain?" she asked.

"Mike and I went fishing today, and Dad's outside on the front porch, sound asleep, I think. We've been gone all day and came back a few minutes ago, so haven't talked to him. We fixed the clogged drain last night. He tried to help but was furious because we wouldn't let him. He sat in his wheelchair and grumbled to himself. He looked like a pathetic old man."

"You fixed it? Thank you. I wanted to call a plumber, but he wouldn't have any part of it. Too much money, he said, and that was the end of that. He's tired and unhappy a lot these days. I think he's having a midlife crisis."

"I thought mid-life crises happened at age forty, not seventy," Jeff commented.

"That's true," Audrey agreed, "this is his second one. You know your father, one-upping everyone and everything, two midlife crises instead of only one. Double."

Lizzy mouthed, *more on Logan. Ask her if she's sleeping with him.*

Jeff brushed her aside and nodded, "So, Mom, what's going on between you and Logan? Are you two dating or something? As far as I know, you've never had a male friend, somebody you hung out with. He's a nice guy, but we're curious."

"Mike asked me the same thing," Audrey replied.

"Mike said you didn't answer, and he thinks you are sleeping with him. Are you?" Jeff asked again.

Audrey paused for a moment, "Aren't you two the snoopy ones, but really, do you think I would betray your dad?"

Jeff stammered, "Well, no, but…"

"Then you've answered your own question," she answered more curtly than she intended. "Sophie and Ava want to bake cookies so I better go. When are you coming home?"

"We're not sure, we didn't catch anything and want to spend a little more time fishing. We don't think it is good to leave Dad alone, so somebody needs to stay with him while we drive back to Huckleberry and you drive home. That's probably a two, maybe three-day turnaround and he can't be by himself that long."

"Call one of the home health agencies and hire someone to stay for a couple days. He'll be fine," she said.

Without thinking, Jeff blurted out, "How about his nurse, Carlee?"

"Carlee? She's not a nurse, she doesn't do anything except yoga. She's the dentist's wife."

CHAPTER 56
Logan

Logan had joined Audrey and her four grandchildren at the park and brought lunches for everyone. They had played on the playground equipment for an hour or more and devoured their hamburgers, French fries, and milkshakes. Ethan, a twelve-year-old boy, had distanced himself from his sister and cousins and was madly punching buttons on his cell phone as the younger girls returned to the playground.

"They ate so fast, I doubt they'll want ice cream," Logan said. "And will they want ice cream after the milkshakes?"

"Clearly, you've forgotten about kids' eating habits. In an hour, they'll want a duplicate of what they've already eaten," Audrey laughed. "These monkeys can eat twice what you and I can, and it all goes toward growing taller. I've been pleading for them to stop growing, but they don't listen, and look how tall they are. I live so far away, so I seldom see them. I miss them and their activities and watching them grow up. When the boys were growing up, we were so busy with the farm that I felt like I hardly saw them some days. And now I see these guys even less. It's not what I had in mind. I need more Grandma time."

"Marry me, and we can move to Huckleberry, and you can see your monkeys every day," Logan offered again. "We could also stay in Portland, where I already own a house, which hasn't been lived in. Or we could become cruisaholics, like Phyllis and Gus. I could sell my house, and we could use the money to cruise. And don't forget that I have a condo in Lauderdale. It's not big, but it's nice. And paid for. I'm not excited about living in Hunter, but if that's what you want, I'll live through it."

"It's not that easy, Logan. It's easy for you because Joan isn't with you any longer, but I'm different. Griff is my husband and he needs me," Audrey replied.

"You keep saying that Griff needs you, but do you need him?" Logan asked. "You've never indicated that at all. I need you, too, Audrey. Now what are you going to do? You have two men who need you," he chuckled, "Yeah, think about that."

The two eight-year olds ran up, "Grandma, can we buy ice cream now? I want rocky road, a big scoop."

"You just ate," I said, "are you hungry already? What did I tell you, Logan, hungry all the time!"

The youngest one said, "I want mint chocolate chip because it's my favorite. Are you and Mr. Logan dating? Daddy thinks you are. I wish you lived closer, Grandma, we could have these play dates every week."

"We'll go for ice cream in a while, go play some more," Audrey told them as they ran off.

"See, they think you should live closer, too. It's unanimous, what about it?"

CHAPTER 57
Audrey

An ice cream parlor sat adjacent to the park, so they ordered ice cream and returned to the nearby benches to finish it. Only the youngest made it to the park before finishing her cone. "Let's go to the phone store," Ethan said. "I'll help you pick out a phone."

Audrey said, "I want the XPhone, so you don't have to help me. I'll just ask for the XPhone. That's what Phyllis has, and she's savvy about technology stuff. Her phone is black, so maybe I'll find a different color, if they have different colors."

"Sheesh, Grandma," Ethan said firmly, "we're going to the XPhone store, so all they sell is XPhones." He rolled his eyes thinking this would be a nightmare trip. "But they'll have all kinds of cool options. You should buy the newest version, and I'll explain everything."

"Okay," Audrey said, hesitantly, wondering what "everything" he was talking about. "They have cameras, which will be fun. And I see people playing games like solitaire, and I might enjoy playing those, particularly when Grandpa is laid up. Other than that, I don't think I need anything."

Logan said, "I have a year old XPhone, and it does everything except wash your dishes, but if you have an electronic dishwasher, you might be able to program it to do that chore, too."

Audrey said, "This sounds expensive, how much are they?"

"It depends on what you want," Ethan said. "Let's find a tech to help you choose what's best for you and Grandpa."

Ethan rounded up a tech person with a white shirt and tie who looked professional, although he looked younger than Ethan, Audrey thought. He said, "Okay, ma'am, let me explain the features, and you can advise me about which ones you like, and we can select exactly the right phone for you."

Audrey thought, *exactly the right phone? How many can there be?* but said, "Yes, help me to select the right one. I've never used one."

"Every phone comes with a camera and a touch screen, so those are givens. I'm going to list some of the most popular new features, and you tell me if they are important to you."

Tech guy began to list, and Audrey responded to each of his options.

Tech guy: *Find my phone?*

Audrey said no, but Logan nodded yes. She looked at him, and he said emphatically, "They are small, and you might lose the phone, and this will help you find it."

"Okay, yes, I'll add that," Audrey agreed hesitantly.

Tech guy: *Falling assist?*

Audrey thought he had misspoken and meant *calling assist* and asked, but tech guy assured her that he meant falling assist, an automatic connection to emergency help if she fell. Audrey shook her head no, but Logan and Ethan chimed together, *yes*. "You live eighteen miles from town, and if you fall, you'll need help. This will automatically notify a service that will call the EMTs. Yes, Grandma, you need this."

"Okay," she consented reluctantly.

Tech guy: *Pedometer and heart rate monitor?*

Audrey perked up. "Pedometer? I walk every day so that would be useful. My old one is about caput anyway. Heart monitor? Maybe. Will it take my temperature?"

Tech guy: *Yes, we can add a thermometer, and the pedometer and heart monitor are one unit. Is that a yes?*

Logan said, "Maybe I should upgrade, I'd like that, too."

Audrey said, "This list is long, but yes."

Tech guy: *Retina display?*

Audrey asked, "What's that for? Does it help with glaucoma?" She was thinking of Griff and his preoccupation with glaucoma.

Tech guy: *Not glaucoma, but it reduces the number of passwords you have to recall.*

Audrey said, "YES!"

Tech guy: *Maps and GPS?*

Audrey said, "I have a road atlas, but forgot to bring it, and I have GPS in my car, but I don't know how to work it."

Logan said, "We used your automobile's GPS on this trip, and it was complicated. This will make it easier for you, so you should add it. Do you remember when our trip was rearranged because of construction? Yes, you need this."

Audrey sighed and said, "Okay."

Then Ava and Sophie chimed in and advised, "Get games, Grandma, lots of games."

Tech guy answered, "They all come with some games, but we can add more for you. No problem. It's easier to do it now than when you are at home, especially if you don't have an XPhone store nearby."

"I'll help you set up your email and social media on this phone," Ethan said.

The tech guy ran through a few more options, and Audrey said yes to most, at Logan's insistence. She added remote access for lights and garage doors, a longer lasting battery, and an enhanced security plan. He showed her several types of headphones, and Logan pushed her toward wireless so she could listen to books as she walked.

The tech guy grabbed her flip phone and snapped it open and shut a few times saying, "Hot potatoes! I haven't seen one of these dinosaurs in about five years. I'll move your contacts from your old phone. Would you like anything else, like a protective case, perhaps?"

The eight-year-old cousins picked out a pink studded rhinestone case that they said was trendy, and she handed it to the tech. "That's all. I don't want to know how much this is, so don't tell me. Put it on the credit card." And can I have a new phone number? I want the Idaho area code but would prefer a number that is easy to remember. She inhaled a deep breath thinking Griff will kill her because she remembered when he talked about making a phone call for one thin dime.

"I have one more question that you haven't mentioned," she said to the tech suddenly.

"What did I leave out?" the tech questioned.

"Does it call people?" she queried. "I just need to make sure."

CHAPTER 58
Phyllis

Gus was on the mend, thank heavens, but Phyllis was confused about Steve. She had tried to send him away, but he continued to show up. He said he was there to console her, but then one thing led to two, which led to two more. She needed to talk to someone, but who? Who would lend a sympathetic ear? Audrey, that's who. She was reasonable and listened and made sense. She was a nurse, and nurses excelled at that type of thing. She must have returned from Oregon by now, so Phyllis decided to drive to their farm, hoping Audrey could give her some advice and talk her through this. Griff would be home, but Audrey would find a place to talk privately.

She pulled into the drive-through and bought four strawberry milkshakes, one for each of them and one to take to Gus later.

When she arrived at Audrey's farm, a new SUV was parked in the driveway, and she wondered whether Audrey had bought a new vehicle while she had been in Oregon. It contained Oregon license plates, but if it were Audrey's, she would have to register it in Idaho. That was the law. Unless it was Logan's rig, and he was back. Carlee had mentioned some time ago that Logan and Audrey were locked together driving what she called the love buggy, but Phyllis dismissed it as Carlee's rumor mill. They were friends, sure, but she didn't think they did anything more than walking their 10,000 steps together. Audrey's was the straightest of straight arrows and wouldn't stray from Griff.

She knocked on the door and was surprised to see Jeff, Audrey's son on the other side of the door. "Jeff! What a surprise," she said. "Do you remember me? I'm Mrs. Gustafson, your twelfth grade English teacher."

"Of course, I remember you, Mrs. Gustafson, you were my BETE," Jeff bragged as he grinned and hugged her. "Best English Teacher Ever. You actually made Macbeth fun."

She laughed at that and said, "TYVM, thank you very much. It's good to see you. We did have fun, didn't we? Is your mom here? I need to see her for a few minutes."

"No, she's babysitting our kids in Oregon. Mike and Abby are here, too. And Lizzy, my wife, although I don't think you've met her. Dad's here though. Would he do?" Jeff asked.

"Sure, I'd like to see your dad, I even brought him a milkshake, but I hoped to see Audrey," she replied. "I have a little problem and want her advice. She's good at sorting things out. How long are you staying in Hunter?"

Jeff explained their schedule, "How's Mr. Gustafson? Dad said he had a heart attack. He was a favorite teacher, too. BPETE, he used to say. Best PE Teacher Ever. We would like to stay a couple more days, but the fish aren't biting. Say, Mrs. G, maybe you can help us, or maybe you'll know someone who can. Dad got banged up on the cruise, as you know, and we need to have someone stay with him until Mom comes home, but we can't find anyone. We don't think he should stay alone. I don't know if you've noticed, but he seems a little strange lately. Do you know anyone who could help us out, you know, sort of babysit Dad till Mom arrives? It'll be three days, a day for us to drive home and two for Mom to drive back here...so three days total. Do you know anybody?"

Babysit Griff, how funny, she thought. He and she had enjoyed each other on the cruise. She was thinking fast. With Gus gone for a few more days, she had plenty of room, and Steve would be less likely to come by if Griff were there, solving her problem with Steve. Griff, in a wheelchair with a cast on his foot, wouldn't be chasing her around the house. "How about me?" she blurted out. "With Gus in the hospital, I'm alone, and I don't have a dog or anything to keep me busy, I could look after Griff until

Audrey comes back to Hunter, but would it be okay to take him to my house? I like being closer to town, and with Gus in the hospital, I don't want to be way out here in the boonies. Besides, my house is empty, and I'm lonely."

"Are you sure? He can be cantankerous, but I don't see anything wrong with that. We can take the wheelchair and throw some duds in a suitcase and he can take a little staycation at my BETE's house. Thank you! It'll be just three days, but we'll want to leave at dawn tomorrow, so we'll take him to your house tonight if that will work for you."

CHAPTER 59
Phyllis

Phyllis' heart was pounding at the thought of being needed once again, to help Griff. The hardest thing about her retirement had been that she wasn't needed any longer. Her students had always needed her for something, for learning of course, but also for hugs or an ear for listening to their problems. Her forty years of teaching students zipped by in a hurry and suddenly she wasn't needed any longer. The new and adventurous things had often filled her void, but those didn't help when a new kind of loneliness set in. Having someone else in the house would remove the vacuous void that echoed in her head each time she came through the door. It unnerved her to be alone, surrounded by space filled with nothing, no conversation, no laughter, no Gus.

But now, she was needed again. Hurrah for her.

Jeff and Mike mentioned that Griff had pitched a fit at the idea of being babysat, but they extricated him from his house and delivered him, wheelchair and all, to Phyllis. He was upset, but didn't fuss to her, because he knew she wouldn't listen to his complaints. She handed Griff a bottle of Gus' favorite beer and steered him to the kitchen table.

"This is a fine thing," Griff said, "thrown out of my own house. I'll stay tonight but tomorrow you can take me back. They think I'm some kind of baby who needed babysitting. They've been ignoring me, like I'm invisible. Talking about me as if I weren't in the room, but I was. It's annoying."

Phyllis agreed, "I understand, Griff, I'm invisible sometimes, too.

When I taught school, my students ignored me. It was like they had gone one hundred percent deaf or that I was one hundred percent mute, and when Gus and I bought a car or appliance or had a repairman, the salesperson or fix-it guy had no idea that I was present. It's my gray hair that makes me fade into the woodwork. Store clerks don't see me patiently standing in line to buy their merchandise and restaurant servers have no idea I am waiting. I appear to have substance when I look in the mirror, but maybe it's my imagination. But I have hope because last week someone gave me the finger while I was driving. I don't know why, but at any rate, I felt validated."

Griff laughed, "That's pretty funny, because I see you fine, and you are a knockout, gray hair and all."

"Griff, you have to heal, and you'll never be better if you continue to walk on your injured feet. I'll be at your beck and call until Audrey comes home."

"Beck and call? Huh. That's not likely, and it's Audrey's job to take care of me, not yours. She's my wife, and it's her job," Griff argued.

"And what's your job?" Phyllis queried. "Your job is to heal, so I'm not returning you to your house. You are going to stay with me and heal."

"Where am I sleeping?"

"I guess with me, because I'm sure not lugging you upstairs, you big oaf," Phyllis said, giving him a quick doughboy poke. He was injured, and she had terminated her new and adventurous things project, but she wondered if their libidos would rise again as they had before.

"Won't that be weird? I mean Gus is in the hospital, and you and I are sleeping in his bed," Griff said.

CHAPTER 60
Audrey

The next morning Lizzy made left-over steak sandwiches while the rest readied themselves for the trip home. It was a long drive, and they would make better time if they didn't have to stop to eat. They could buy drinks at the local convenience store before leaving town. They debated whether to call Audrey to inform her they would be returning home a couple days early but decided against it. If she and Logan were together, their suspicions would be confirmed. With any luck, they would arrive home after the kids were in bed, and maybe find Audrey and Logan in a rapturous clench.

Abby was relieved, "I'm happy Mrs. Gustafson volunteered to help with Griff. I like her and she's a social person and needs company. It's only for three days and Mr. G will be released from the hospital soon. Even if Griff is in a sour mood, it will better than an empty house. I loved Mrs. G's classes. Enjoyed Mr. G, too."

Lizzy agreed, "I'm glad he's at her house, so he'll be away from that hooker-like nurse, Carlee. Audrey told Jeff that she was the dentist's wife, but I'm sure she was wearing the nurse's uniform that we bought Audrey for Christmas a while back. Carlee looked like a hooker in it. And now Griff is writing love notes and watching SXTV. This is not the Griff we know and sort of love."

Mike let out a chuckle, "Yeah, this is definitely not Dad, especially the poetry part. I doubt he could do more than a *roses are red* poem."

Jeff added, "Mrs. Gustafson's a good person, and Dad's in good hands,

165

but what about Logan? And Mom? What do we do about them?"

Lizzy shook her head, "Jeff, we don't do anything about them. Mom's smart, and none of us knows what she's thinking or where her heart is. She said they weren't sleeping together, so we have to trust that they are BFFs and nothing more."

Mike countered, "Not exactly, she avoided the question each time we asked, and we must have asked it three or four times. Mom's hiding something, or she would be denying it. She's not saying, and so I'm betting they're doing it."

Lizzy said, "I have a novel idea: Why don't we sit down with Mom and Logan and talk it through. Why not tell us if they are having a fling, but she's easy to read and among the four of us, we should be able to figure it out."

Jeff's SUV pulled into Mike's driveway several hours later. The kids were already tucked away, and Audrey was spellbound with a book while sipping a glass of red wine. She didn't hear them pull up and jumped when they opened the door, "Oh, you're home, you said you were fishing all week. I'm glad to see you, but is everything all right with Griff? Is he out of the wheelchair?" Her emotions had spent the week zigzagging among guilt, fear, happiness, sorrow, euphoria. It had been worse than hot flashes.

Mike said, "The fish weren't biting, and we decided to come home a couple days early because we were worried about you. You sounded tired and these guys can wear you out." He gestured to the second floor where the kids would be asleep.

"It's been a difficult week, all right. Between worrying about Griff and caring for the kids, I didn't have a lot of spare time. Luckily, Logan helped me," Audrey commented, wondering if she had said too much.

Mike answered, "He stayed here? With you? In our house? Mom, what were you thinking?"

"Why would you worry about your mom? She's fine," someone said from the direction of the kitchen. They turned around and dropped their jaws as Logan appeared in the doorway with an apron around his waist and wiping his hands with a towel. He shook their hands, "Good to see you, again. How was the trip? I didn't hear you come in because I was straightening up the kitchen."

Audrey said, "Logan brought us dinner tonight. A roast. I'm sure we have some left over. Are you hungry?"

CHAPTER 61
Logan

Mike glared at Logan with angry eyes. "What are you doing here? Have you been here the whole time we were gone? I want to talk to you."

Abby said, "Mike, calm down. He's visiting, as your mom said, and he brought dinner and cleaned the kitchen. I'm all in favor of him moving in permanently! Thank you, Logan."

Logan gave a little bow and tipped an absent hat, "My pleasure, Miss Abby."

Audrey snapped, "Oh, Mike, for pity's sake, what's with you? Can you not behave yourself? Nothing is going on between Logan and me, we are friends that's all. And you haven't told me about your father." Audrey was hoping to change the subject. Mike was bullheaded like Griff, and she knew he wouldn't back off. Jeff was easier to deal with, but not tonight.

Jeff announced, "I agree with Mike. I'd like to talk to Logan, to see what's going on. To find out why he is so attentive to you, Mom."

Logan had been standing in the doorway, trying to figure out what to say, if he were to say anything at all. He watched Audrey welling back her tears and moved toward her and put his arm around her and squeezed. He whispered, "Showtime." Audrey gasped, not knowing what he meant. Fearful of what he would say, she could hardly breathe. Her life as she knew it was over, no matter what he said, and if he told the truth, the boys would kill Logan and bury him in the woodpile or throw him in the river or some other fate worse than death.

"What are you going to say?" she murmured back in his ear.

Mike said, "What the H are you two whispering about? All this secrecy is what I'm talking about."

Logan continued to embrace Audrey, and she didn't brush him back, so without more hesitation, he answered, "I'll tell you what's going on because it's time you knew. I'm crazy in love with your mom and have told her so multiple times." Mike and Jeff sat down hard in the nearest chairs and Abby and Lizzy grinned and pumped *yes* with their fists.

Mike said, "I knew it. I knew it. And you're sleeping together, aren't you? Did you sleep together here? In my house?"

Logan knew Audrey would kill him if he told the truth, "No, but not for lack of trying. While I am persistent, she has a confounded, stubborn, moral streak in her brain that she won't release. Therefore, we are remaining friends, merely friends. I wish things were different, but they aren't. She's married to your dad, and as far as I know, she intends to stay with him. Any questions?"

Mike looked at Jeff. "Do we have questions?"

Jeff said, "I'm sure we do, but I am so stunned that I'm not sure I can put them together."

Audrey was fuming and didn't hold back. She said, "Well, I don't have a question, but I do have a comment, as long as we're throwing my life away. Your dad resents Logan and wants him gone, but he's my friend, perhaps the best friend I've ever had, and you both need to quit nosing around and let me live my life. I'll deal with your dad, so you don't need to tell him anything about this discussion. Got it?"

Abby and Lizzy continued grinning, and Abby said, "Go for it, Audrey. You've earned happiness and if you and Logan want to be friends or more than friends, you have our vote and none of us will stop you, right Mike? Right Jeff?"

Logan released her from his grasp and raised his eyebrows. "You heard the lady, yes, we are friends. Friends. BFFs as they say in textland."

Mike said, "It won't work. Men and women cannot be friends. It's a rule. A hard and fast rule."

Lizzy jumped in, "Not true, Mike, lots of women have male friends. Just because you don't, doesn't mean it can't happen. And with your dad the way he is, Logan and Audrey's friendship is wonderful. Your dad can be a royal pain in the behind, and Audrey has never been free to do what she wants. It is fine."

"What do you mean, *the way he is?*" Audrey asked. "You said he was fine."

"He seems accident prone," Jeff answered, "and maybe he's going through male menopause, but he seems obsessed with thoughts about sex. That's new, right? He's never done that before, has he? He was watching SXTV and trying to write poetry, for hell's sake. That's not like him at all."

Audrey laughed, "Poetry? Your dad is writing poetry? I don't think so. And by the way, why did you think that Carlee was a nurse? She and her husband, Steve, moved to Hunter from Salt Lake and joined us on the cruise. Steve is a dentist, but she's not a nurse. Definitely not a nurse."

Jeff continued, "Dad told us she was a nurse, and she had this nurse's uniform on, which was short, like a mini-mini skirt. Her butt and boobs hung out. She was there when we arrived."

Lizzy chimed in, "I thought she was a hooker because, well, she looked like a hooker, her uniform, her makeup, her hair. But I think she was wearing one of your nurse's uniforms, the one we gave you the Christmas before you retired."

"My uniform? That's weird. Friday was Carlee's day to check on Griff, so that explains why she was at our house, but I don't know about the uniform. Who knows why Carlee does anything?" Audrey asked with no expectation of an answer.

CHAPTER 62
Audrey

"Listen, guys, I'm exhausted and would like to go to bed, but I'm going to stay at Logan's, if that's okay with him. I need a good night's sleep before we set out for Hunter tomorrow. Logan is going to drive with me. We had a horrendous trip coming to Huckleberry, and although you didn't have trouble, I'm not prepared for a repeat performance of Buster, the car thief, and deer leaping over my car if I'm alone. We'll let you know what time we are leaving and drop by first so that I can kiss everybody goodbye."

Mike flared up, "You're staying with HIM? Mom, this is going too far."

"Yes, I am going to stay with HIM. He has a big house with several rooms and several beds, and we can either orgy all night, or I'll behave my lustful self and not *do the dirty*, a term you gleaned from your dad, Mike," Audrey said.

Logan wiggled his eyebrows and began to chuckle, saying, "I can dream, can't I."

Mike and Jeff scowled, and Abby began to giggle, "She nailed it, Mike, that's what you say, sometimes. She nailed it."

Audrey gathered up her new suitcase and clothes as well as a couple books and her new phone, and she and Logan went to her car. "That wore me out. I was already tired from all the activities, the park, and phone buying, but now this. The fox is in the chicken coop, so what if Griff finds out, which he will for sure. What if he kills me? Or you?"

"They were less angry than I expected them to be. Mike was angry,

171

but I'm not sure if it was at me or that you and I have secrets. Abby and Lizzy are on my team, but I'm not so sure about Jeff. He's concerned for Griff and worried he will wear you out. Your monkeys were a handful, but Griff is a lot more demanding than they are, Audrey. Griff is more than a handful," Logan said.

The what ifs began pouring out of her, "What if Griff has more injuries? And what if he hates me? He's their grandfather. And he's still my…husband." Audrey was speaking but Logan did a voice over on the word *husband*.

"Yes, and he needs you, and you have vows and plenty of what ifs. Nobody knows what tomorrow will bring, and I have a few what ifs for you: What if you spent your next fifteen or fifty years happier than you ever have been in your first sixty-seven? What if you were treated like a princess every day instead of a housekeeper and love slave? What if I love you more than Griff ever loved you or is capable of? Those are the what ifs I can offer."

Audrey didn't answer but began aimlessly chewing her lip on their way back to Portland, accumulating a whole new list of what ifs that remained unspoken. What if she divorced Griff and married Logan, and it didn't work out? What if Logan expected more than she could give sexually? What if Logan's daughters didn't like her? What if her kids wouldn't accept Logan? What if Griff wouldn't give her a divorce, and what if she had to spend the next years in Hunter with Griff after she told him she loved Logan?

Loved Logan, she repeated in her mind. Did she? She thought of that last sentence. Did she love Logan? That was question number one. Question number two was whether she remained in love with Griff? She had loved him forever, even before she met him, she had told people. But now with Logan, she had doubts about her love toward Griff. It wasn't the same love. Griff was solid, did all the right things, but he had never excited her emotionally or physically like Logan did. And Griff had a few flaws, things that drove her crazy, and those flaws had deepened and widened, but he was a good man and a good husband and father, she thought, and she used to consider herself fortunate to be married to him. She liked Logan, liked everything about him and couldn't think of a flaw, except maybe he was over persistent in his quest for her, but was that a flaw or an asset? Why didn't she have a measuring stick for love?

"Why isn't there a measuring stick for love?" she repeated to Logan as they drove into his garage. "I need a measuring stick because I don't think I know what love is anymore."

They exited the Lexus but remained in the garage when Logan pulled her close saying "Let's try this, I'm going to give you a measuring stick, Audrey," he paused. "Not the kind you think," he paused again, smiling, "but rather, I'm going to kiss you. I want you to take account of your emotions because afterwards I want you to tell me how you feel, from your sexy little toes to the top of your pointy little head."

He kissed her long and hard and when they pulled away, Audrey was panting. Her eyes twinkled and grew large, and her cheeks flushed. Logan asked, "Well, Princess, how was it?"

"Toe-gasm," she gasped, "knee-gasm, foo-foo-gasm, elbow-gasm. I didn't think I had a pointy head, but if I do, it has a gasm, too. Oh, Logan, if these gasms are a measuring stick for love, I'm toe over pointy head in love with you. Yes, Logan, I love you."

CHAPTER 63
Audrey

When they entered the house, Audrey thought that Logan would wrestle her to bed, as she was aroused, and she was sure he was, as well, but he surprised her. "You are going to bed, and by going to bed, I mean to sleep. I can see how exhausted you are, and I have no intention of taking advantage of your weariness. You said you love me, but I want to make sure that you love me, not my over-hormoned, sexy, male body," he chuckled. "Let's go upstairs, and you can sleep in the guest room again, but not too many more times. If your sons followed us home, they won't find us doing anything except catching Z's, not the hula, as Phyllis says." Logan helped her into her nightgown, never touching her. He tucked her in bed and kissed her on her forehead. "I'll be downstairs. Sleep well, my love."

Audrey's life was turning upside down and she wrestled with herself to sleep. Once she fell into slumber, though, she was down for the count, sleeping far later than she had intended. She had hoped to return to Hunter that day. When she finally rallied, she found Logan at the kitchen table finishing his crossword puzzles and drinking a bottle of water.

"Finally, the princess awakens," Logan said. "What wanteth thou for thy morning, rather, noon meal?"

"I didn't mean to sleep so late," Audrey said. "I was worn out. Kids are hard work. I don't want to have any more children."

"No problem, I'll wear a condom," Logan returned. "I promise, but I doubt I have any little Logans jumping around inside me."

"I've been going through menopause for about twenty-five years, so I don't think it'll be a problem for me either" Audrey shuddered. *What am I thinking, I told him I loved him last night, and now I'm talking about having his children? Oh, dear God. What about Griff?*

Logan scrambled four eggs, nuked four slices of bacon, and popped bread in the toaster, and in less than five minutes, they sat across from each other eating.

"I want to see my monkeys before we start our trip to Hunter. We won't make it all the way to Hunter tonight, but with any luck, we won't see the Hidden Garden Inn. But maybe we should bring a few of our own towels on the trip, just in case," she joked.

***

Abby was home and met her at the door when they drove in. "Mike calmed down after you left. He was hot for a while, but Jeff, Lizzy, and I talked to him. We understand how you are feeling, Audrey. You've been with Griff a long time, and he's become difficult, and it's hard to think about a change. You have a lot of life left in you, and Logan is nice, and I am finding I like him, more than Griff. I sometimes called Griff "Gruff" because he could be gruff. I'll keep Mike on a low burner. He wants you happy, but he's worried about what will happen to Griff if you leave him."

All four of her monkeys came in the room, and the three girls surrounded and hugged Audrey. She warned, "Don't grow up while I'm gone. Stay as you are, I'll be back soon." Ethan held back, then shook her hand.

"How about you, Dr. Logan, will you be back soon, too?" Ava asked. "Are you gonna be our new grandpa?"

CHAPTER 64
Phyllis

Phyllis felt awkward about Griff sleeping in her bed, but she knew Griff couldn't maneuver the stairs, so she had no choice. She didn't want to sleep upstairs either, so she waited until Griff had zonked out before crawling into the bed next to him. He twitched a few times, and she thought he might wake up, but he didn't. He was not quite snoring, and she had to admit, a warm male body lying next to her sent her goosebumps. An hour after she lay down beside him, he put his arm over her and pulled her close. She didn't know if he was awake or not, but it felt good. Her heart quickened, and she felt frisky, but she remembered Gus and buried that thought.

She rose early the next morning, not knowing what Griff and she would do all day. She would make a visit to see Gus, but after that, she wasn't sure. Gus and Phyllis' life together had been easy: They waltzed through their daily routines, spent some time conversing about everything and nothing, always enjoying each other. Even after forty years together, they flirted with daily teasing or cooing. In hindsight, Phyllis questioned why she started her new and adventurous things project because she loved Gus, and he was all she needed.

Griff came out of the bedroom, "I've been calling Audrey all morning and she doesn't answer. I don't know what's going on," he grumbled, speed-dialing her again. "It keeps saying her phone was disconnected and I'm tired of all this nonsense. She needs to be home where she can help me."

"Maybe the cell towers are out. She'll call, be patient. Let me fix you some breakfast," Phyllis offered. "Bacon and eggs, are you hungry? Why don't you call Jeff or Mike? Maybe she called them."

"They won't be any help. They're the ones who dumped me here. I need Audrey," Griff insisted.

Griff was the most unromantic person Phyllis had ever met and her mind raced, seeking a brilliant idea to help him become more romantic. If he could become more romantic, Audrey might show him more attention, and he would be happier, and she would have a better chance of keeping her recent vows about being faithful to Gus. It didn't take long before she thought of exactly the right idea. She had been successful in her new and adventurous things project, and perhaps she could transfer some of those skills to Griff. She was excited at the opportunity to have a new project. As an effective teacher, Griff would be putty in her hands.

"I've been mulling over ideas about how to spend today, Griff, and I figured it out. You are going to school. You are going to enroll in Phyllis' Academy of Romance, and I'll give you a crash course on how to be romantic. I'm going to teach you everything I know, and Audrey will be wild over the new Griff," she informed him, delighting at the thought that this could be a pleasurable way to pass the day with Griff.

"I don't need school. I've been thinking about what you said about romance and I've already figured it out," Griff griped. "I've even practiced writing poems."

She said, "Today, you don't have Audrey, you have me, so you are going to pretend that I'm Audrey. So what are we going to do? Shall we go on a picnic or go for a drive? Or maybe even visit a new winery? Let's do something," she said. "Something fun. What would you like to do with Audrey if she walked in right now?"

"Do with Audrey? You know, what she loves to do: *the dirty*, she begs for it," Griff chortled. "What woman doesn't? I don't want to go for a drive, I'll rest my foot today, stay home."

"Let me ask another way, what would Audrey like to do with you?"

"I don't know, I never know what she wants to do. Go for a walk and read a book. Talk to Lo…gan." He drawled it out, mocking Audrey.

"Okay, you clearly aren't getting this, Griff, so let's start with the basics. The ABC's of romance. I'm an expert, and you can practice on me. For Audrey," Phyllis said.

"Well, okay, if you think it will keep her out of Quack's clutches."

"First, you are going to hold my hand, just hold it, like you are madly in love with my hand. It's the hand of your dreams, the one and only hand in the world, and you are crazy for it," she said.

Griff picked up her hand and used it to rub his leg, inching her hand toward his crotch.

"No, no. What are you doing, Griff? Hold my hand, like this." She picked up his hand with both of hers and began massaging it, one knuckle at a time. After a few minutes, she was a little turned on herself and asked, "How does that feel?"

Griff had relaxed his eyes shut and grunted a moan, "Good, relaxing, making my worries go away."

"Does it turn you on?" she asked.

"It might if you keep it up. You and I *did the dirty* one time, on the ship, do you remember? I definitely remember, and I liked it and I think you liked it, too. You do know how to turn a fellow on, Phyllis, that's for sure."

She shook her head as she had at many students through the years, "Before we go any farther, Griff, you have to stop saying *doing the dirty*. We already talked about this. You have to stop using it because it sounds like it's something bad, soiled, rotten, and it's not. Sex is pure and wonderful, so I don't want to hear *doing the dirty* again. From now on, we are going to call it *rowing the love boat* or *rowing Audrey's love boat*. Got it? It's a fun term, not stained or grimy."

"I've always called it *doing the dirty*, but if you think Audrey will like it better, I'll try to change," Griff said. "Hey, Phyllis, do you want to row the love boat?" He chortled at his comment.

"Griff, you're impossible, so now, back to my hand. I want you do the same to me, caress and massage my hand. And if you master those, we'll add ear nibbles followed by some neck effects, little ear blows, gentle puffs that will leave Audrey wanting more. But first, make me desire you through some tender hand caresses," Phyllis scolded. Griff surprised her with soft and gentle strokes, so soothing that her foo-foo began to launch into meltdown mode. He began the ear nibbles without prompting, which was encouraging, followed by neck puffs that sent major messages to her libido. She began to think this might not have been a good idea, particularly because she had sworn to abandon her bracelet project. However, Griff was doing well, and she didn't want to discourage him, so she decided she should add another move, but what? She thought maybe a quick and innocent kiss would be a pleasant addition, so she said, "Kiss me, Griff." Her voice dropped an octave and came out huskier than it had been ten minutes before, and their kiss was neither innocent nor quick.

Their clothes started leaving their bodies, and in seconds they lay in a heap on the floor. Griff was massaging more than just her hands, and she melted at his touch. She should have said *stop*, but her body said *go*, so they went, and she felt strangely attracted to Griff.

Sex with Gus as a young man had brought her to life, but the new and adventurous things encounters were merely sex without emotional attachment and were meaningless, other than adding a charm to her bracelet. Gus' libido expired two years prior, and although the bracelet project was bold and exciting at the time, she had dismissed her random partners and events from her mind the minute they were over, and she had attached a new charm.

She had dismissed the shipboard encounter with Griff as meaningless, like the others, but today, it was different, romantic and passionate, and she cherished his presence. Griff had figured out the romance part of sex, and it had warmed her, no, more than that, it had heated her up, brought her back to life, she felt desired. She didn't know why and wondered if Griff felt the same way.

She increased her curriculum for the next two days and added classes on poetry, foot rubs, love notes, cuddling, and spontaneous behavior. He perfected the art of nibbling, ear blowing, and hand massages rapidly, and he taught her a few things about kissing. He was a good kisser, she had to admit. She gave him A+ on everything, except poetry, which was going to take some work.

CHAPTER 65
Griff

On the third afternoon, after two days of intense romance instruction, Phyllis suddenly said, "Griff, I need a break. Let's go for a walk. You've been an amazing learner, but I think we've gone overboard in our lessons. It's a beautiful day, so let's go outside. We can work on how to take a romantic walk through the park."

"Do I have to walk, or can we take the wheelchair because all this romance instruction has about done me in. Your classes are active, Phyllis, almost too much. No wonder Gus had a heart attack."

"Sure. The park isn't far, just a few blocks, and I'll push you. The city planted a rose garden last year, and the roses are just now coming into bloom, and they are worth the trip."

Phyllis pushed the wheelchair, and Griff rode to the city's rose garden, and it was beautiful. All colors and types of roses were budding and in bloom, as well as yellow and purple irises sticking their heads out of their stalks. Phyllis found an empty bench where she could rest, and they sat together enjoying the ambience and sights and smells of the roses. "Griff, this would be something Audrey would like. You can bring her here and buy her some ice cream and enjoy the peaceful silence of the rose garden. She would love it."

"What the...?" Griff swatted at his neck and shouted, "No, allergy, I'm allergic to bees," as he continued to swat himself, leaned forward, and collapsed onto the paved patio.

Phyllis picked up her handbag and air-smacked at the giant wasp twice, but it reversed direction and aimed itself dead on at her. and she gave it all she had, stunning it on her third try, and it fell to the ground. She stepped on it and ground it beneath her shoe.

She looked at Griff, whose neck had already puffed up double its usual size, and he was not moving. She looked in her purse for her cell phone, which was missing. She called to a passerby, "Call 911, he's allergic and not moving. He might be dead."

The EMTs arrived within a few minutes but couldn't revive Griff. His allergy was severe, and the sting of the wasp, a killer wasp, Phyllis learned from the EMTs, had closed down his airways. He couldn't breath, and they couldn't resuscitate him.

"I've killed him, I've killed Griff. I didn't mean to, we wanted to go for a romantic walk, that's all." Her tears opened up as the EMTs folded up their gear and placed Griff on a gurney.

CHAPTER 66
Audrey

Audrey and Logan drove to Hunter in no kind of hurry. The monkey-kins had been a full-time job for Audrey, and she was glad to be on her way home. She loved them dearly, but they were a handful. She and Logan opted for dine-in restaurants and ate leisurely meals both days, stopping to read historical road signs that were scattered along the highway. They spent the night at a high-end hotel in Boise and even enjoyed the spa. Definitely not the Hidden Garden, and towels came with the room. The highway overlapped and crisscrossed the Oregon Trail with plenty of planted signs. The sooner they arrived back in Hunter, the sooner she would have to face Griff and make her decision and she was in no hurry for either of those.

She had not heard from Griff and that worried her. He didn't often carry his cell phone, so she tried the landline several times, but he didn't answer. Where could he be? Her mind went wild with more what ifs. What if he had fallen? What if he were dead or hurt and couldn't get to the phone?

Logan and Audrey arrived in Hunter late in the afternoon. She had been away for nine days, a far shorter amount of time than the fourteen days she had anticipated. Griff's pickup sat in the driveway with the keys perched on the visor. The door was unlocked, and she and Logan entered, checking every room, but Griff was nowhere to be seen, and her calls to Griff were met with silence. A large bowl of pasta salad sat in the refrigerator along with an unopened bottle of red wine on the table.

Griff's cell phone was gone, but the sink was clog-free, just as Lizzy had said, and that was a relief. Other than that, nothing had changed since she had left a week earlier. Nothing in the house had changed, that is, because she had changed entirely.

She called Griff's cell phone, but it went to voice mail, so she left a message. Logan suggested, "Let's wait for a while. Maybe someone drove him to town for groceries or something. He'll be back."

"Griff and Bill Sage sometimes visit back and forth; I'll call our neighbor Rosemary Sage. Maybe she knows," Audrey said.

"Audrey, you're back," Rosemary greeted, "I'm glad because I'm worried about Griff. Today was our day to check on him, but I couldn't find him. I left him a bottle of wine and a large bowl of pasta salad, but he was nowhere to be seen. Where is he?"

"I have no idea. I'm wondering the same thing," Audrey said. She clicked off.

Logan suggested, "Let me call the hospital. He might be sick or hurt."

"Wouldn't someone have called me?" Audrey protested, "Oh, cripes, I changed my phone number. That's why Griff hasn't called."

"I didn't think about that. I'll call the hospital anyway," Logan repeated as he started dialing.

Audrey began calling everyone she knew. She wished she had taken advantage of the phone store's offer to transfer all her numbers, but they advised her that she would be charged extra, so she resisted, insisting it was something she could do herself. Her new XPhone seemed complicated, and she needed to learn how to utilize all of its features, so she reasoned that entering the phone numbers herself was a way for her to begin to do so. Now, however, she was having to reenter them from memory or the multiple scraps of paper that she had posted on the refrigerator. Penny wise and pound foolish.

Logan phoned the hospital, but no Griff. Audrey called Steve and Carlee, no Griff. She considered calling Phyllis, but Audrey knew Phyllis would be at the hospital with Gus, and it would be a senseless call.

Audrey knew her sons had both returned to their jobs, as was Lizzy, so finally, not knowing what else to do, she called Abby, "Griff has vanished, he's nowhere to be seen and I'm worried sick. Could you have Mike call me?"

"Sure, Audrey, no problem, but did you check with Mrs. G? Didn't Mike or Jeff tell you? We didn't think it was a good idea for Griff to be left alone, so we searched for someone to stay with him, although he wasn't happy. But Mrs. G. dropped by and volunteered to take care of him, but only if he stayed at her house, rather than yours because it's so far from the hospital. With Mr. G in the hospital, she said it would be easier. Griff blew a gasket about going to her house, but Mike and Jeff insisted and drove him anyway. That's probably where he is. We're going to Jeff and Lizzy's tonight for dinner, so why don't you call us then?"

Audrey dialed Phyllis, but it went to voice mail. She tried Griff with the same result.

Logan had no better luck calling the hospital.

CHAPTER 67
Audrey

It was nearly dark, but Audrey and Logan decided to drive the eighteen miles to town. They hadn't eaten since lunch and had tasted the pasta salad that had been left, but it didn't appeal to them. Audrey wrote her new phone number down on a scratch of paper and asked that Griff call when he arrived home.

They first stopped at Phyllis and Gus' house, but no one answered the door. Audrey thought they might be visiting Gus, so stop number two was the hospital. Gus, dressed in a hospital gown and bathrobe, had a baseball cap perched on his head, and looked healthier than he had since they had met. He was eating saltine crackers and drinking water.

Audrey said, "We're looking for Griff, have you seen him? My daughter-in-law said Phyllis was taking care of him, but we can't find them, and no one's at your house."

Phyllis had just left and was heading home, and they had probably passed her in the elevator, but Gus didn't want to be the bearer of bad news, saying, "No, I haven't seen either of them. Call her in a while. Maybe she went to dinner or something. She likes The Purple Fox, so maybe give it a try. Steve and Carlee like it, too."

"Logan and I want to eat dinner, so we can grab a bite and go back to your house to try to find them. Griff's been with her for three days, and I'm sure he's ready to come home. Phyllis is probably ready for him to be gone, too. You recall the old adage about fish and visitors, both smelling after three days."

Guests filled The Purple Fox to capacity, and the music and guests loomed loud and energetic. Logan spied Steve and Carlee's Volvo in the parking lot, as well as Phyllis' Cruze.

"We're in luck," Audrey said, "Griff and Phyllis are here."

Logan and Audrey anticipated meeting Griff in an angry snit, but they found no Griff, only Steve, Carlee, and Phyllis. Phyllis and Carlee's cheeks were striped with mascara, and Steve was mopping his eyes with his napkin. Uneaten plates of food sat in front of them. Phyllis approached Audrey and said, "I killed him, and I'm so sorry, Audrey. I only wanted to help, and I did it for you." She hugged Audrey, saying, "Don't hate me. I didn't mean anything."

Logan said, "What are you talking about? Where's Griff? Who'd you kill, Phyllis?"

Audrey looked from person to person wondering what was going on. Was Griff dead? That couldn't be.

"Griff, I killed Griff," Phyllis sobbed. "He was desperate to have you back, away from Logan, and wanted to be more romantic, but didn't know how, so I wanted to show him a few tricks, you know to help him, and we went to the park, and this wasp flew by and stung him on the throat and then it came after me, and I squashed it, and he couldn't breath and the EMTs came and I didn't have a phone and then…Oh, Audrey I'm so sorry."

Audrey sat down hard on a chair and Logan followed. Audrey said, "Griff's allergic to bees, but I didn't think a bee sting would kill him. That can't be true, Phyllis, Griff can't be dead. You would never kill anyone, and Griff wanted to be more romantic? He's never said that to me."

Now tears poured down Audrey's cheeks, and Logan put his arms around her. He said, "He's gone, dead? When did this happen?"

Steve answered, "Today, a little while ago. They took him to the Big Pine morgue on the other side of town. I can show you where it is if you like."

Audrey's mind and heart flooded with random emotions, sorrow, anger, angst. She needed to call her sons but didn't think she could.

Maybe Logan could, although that would be bad, they would think he killed Griff.

Logan ordered a bottle of wine and offered Audrey a large glass, which he placed in front of her, but she didn't touch it. He refilled the glasses for everyone at the table as they sat in silence. Finally, Steve said, "Let's toast Griff, he was a great friend, a great farmer, and I, for one, am sorry he's gone." Everyone raised their glasses, but no one except Carlee drank the toast.

Audrey sat in silence for a long time, finally saying, "I need…I need to see Griff, but that can wait until tomorrow. Right now, I need to go home. Would someone take me home, please? I'll call you tomorrow."

Phyllis said, "I'll take you home, Audrey."

Logan offered, "I think it's best if I take Audrey home, but thank you, Phyllis."

CHAPTER 68
Audrey

Audrey was glad for Logan's company although both were lost in their own thoughts and neither of them spoke for the entire trip to the farm. Audrey started to say something once, but no words exited her mouth. The same for Logan, his heart lived for Audrey, but this wasn't how he wanted things to be resolved, and he remained speechless. They had spent much of the past week together, Logan had pursued her, announced his love for her, and now she didn't have a husband, but what did that mean for him? What did it mean for her?

Logan found an unopened bottle of Scotch and poured himself a large portion. Audrey watched him, and nodded and he poured her a portion, too, smaller than his but more than she would usually drink. They drank it in silence.

"My kids, I have to tell Mike and Jeff, and I have to do it tonight, but I'm not sure I can. I can't stop crying for more than a minute, can't think, haven't seen Griff, don't really know what happened, other than Phyllis' disjointed comments. I don't know what to do."

"I can call them," Logan started to say, but Audrey interrupted, "No, that won't do at all. They don't trust either of us, especially you, so that won't work."

"Then who?" Logan asked. "Steve or Carlee? No, they don't know your sons. Phyllis or Gus? No, Phyllis said she killed Griff so she can't call, and Gus is hospitalized. I can't think of anyone else."

"How about the police?" Audrey offered. "They do death notices, don't they?"

Logan answered, "No, not the police. That would scare them, so how about we both do it? You dial the phone, and we'll put it on speaker. Your new phone has the speaker phone feature. Abby said they would all be together tonight, and they are expecting a call to tell them you arrived home okay. I'll help you. I agree that you need to tell them tonight."

Audrey gulped a big swig of Scotch and took a deep breath, praying she could live through the next few minutes, and dialed Mike but Jeff answered.

"Mike, this is Mom. I arrived home okay, nothing exciting on the trip."

"No, this is Jeff, Mike's getting a beer. We're glad to hear it," Jeff responded. "How did Mrs. G make out with Dad? He had a fit about going to stay with her, but we thought it was a good idea. He's bullheaded but has become frail and maybe accident prone. He's never listened to anyone about anything, but Mrs. G was a good teacher and if she could handle Mike and me, she can handle Dad."

"Yes, leaving Dad with Mrs. Gustafson was a good idea, but that's not why I called. Something went wrong," Audrey said.

"Is he all right?' Jeff asked. "I'm going to put you on speaker so everyone can hear."

"Where are the monkeys? Are they in bed?" Audrey asked, hoping they had gone to bed and had fallen asleep. They didn't need to hear this news over the phone.

"Hi Mom," Lizzy called out. The kids are in bed, they miss you."

"I miss them, too, can't wait to see them again," Audrey said, her voice cracking.

"Dad? Is he okay?" Mike called out.

Audrey's voice cracked again, "No, he's not, and I'm not sure how to tell you this."

Mike said, "Are you with Logan again? Damn, Mom, can't you think of Dad instead of Logan?"

"This is Logan, Mike and Jeff. We're on speaker phone. We have bad news; actually, terrible news, and your mom is crying. Your dad was stung by a wasp today, and he died. I'm sure you remember that he was extremely allergic. The venom swelled up his throat, and he couldn't breathe and died immediately. Phyllis was with him. She had taken him to the park to check out the roses. Phyllis told us that she thinks she killed him, but if his allergy were as bad as your mom says it was, no one could have done anything to help. He should have been carrying an EpiPen, but evidently refused the doctor's recommendation."

The phone went silent on both ends until Jeff said, "How about Mom, is she all right?"

"Physically, she's fine, but it was a shock and right now her emotions are like a roller coaster. I'll call her doctor for a prescription of sleeping pills. Hopefully, someone can bring them out, but if they can't I'll go to town for them. I'm going to stay with her until you arrive, but don't worry, I'll sleep on the couch until you get here. I love her but I'm not going to take advantage of her. I'm not seventeen, and neither is she."

CHAPTER 69
Audrey

Audrey felt empty. Griff was dead, and the boys and their families lived in Oregon. Logan stayed with her in Hunter, but respectfully leaving her alone as she tried to come to grips with Griff's demise. As she had told Logan, it was complicated, perhaps even more complicated now that Griff was gone.

She was exhausted and crawled into bed, but her brain immediately snapped to attention, and she remembered a thousand things she had to do. She was a widow. A widow. And she would be completely alone now. She compiled a disorganized list in her cluttered mind of the widows she knew, unraveling how they dealt with the grief that was consuming her. They all reacted differently; some sought adventure, going places and doing things that they never dreamed of doing when their spouses were alive. They traveled or went back to college, became mountain climbers, ran for political office, or involved themselves with exercise programs. Some even had affairs. Several websites specialized in clients for those *over fifty-five*. And Audrey was well over fifty-five. She smiled as she thought of those women who had affairs, because she had a jump on them, she was already having an affair. Wasn't she? Those widows restarted their lives, often improving on the first years.

Others, less fortunate in her mind, succumbed to living a life of loneliness and sadness. They saw their spouse's demise as the end of their lives and never did anything for themselves or their loved ones again. They bought a good television and found the library and played cards once a week. They gave way to health issues and boredom and found themselves early graves or grew even lonelier as their social groups diminished.

Some widows were lonely, some angry, and some felt guilty. Audrey didn't know which she would be, but right now, she felt demolished.

Logan was a widower; his wife had died four years prior and what did he do? He worked for a couple years before leaving Portland to see the world. He was healthy, had ample money, and was smart, with plenty of charisma. And he said that he loved her.

As Audrey saw it, she was sitting at an intersection and needed to determine which direction to go. She suddenly remembered Morgan Freeman's character in Stephen King's *Shawshank Redemption* saying, *you can get busy living or get busy dying.* She knew she needed to get busy living and wanted to start as soon as possible.

She looked at the clock, barely past midnight. She slipped out of bed and headed to the living room, touring the house she knew well, taking account of everything, walls, knickknacks, doors, doorknobs, windows, and lamps. The house looked tired, and after forty-eight years, it had earned that right. Everywhere she looked, she saw Griff. She crept up the stairs and looked at the bedrooms and bath that the boys had used, ignoring the one with the closed door where Logan was sleeping.

She crawled back into bed and closed her eyes again, but they popped open immediately. Logan had once said the only bad decision was no decision, so she needed to decide. She sat up in bed and knew what she had to do.

She sprang out of bed, threw on her robe again and dashed upstairs, but this time she went into the Logan's room, intending to wake him, except he wasn't sleeping either. He was sitting up in bed with a book propped up in front of him. "Audrey, what's going on? Can't you sleep? I heard you prowling around a few minutes ago. Are you okay?"

"Yes, well, no, I think so, maybe, but I'm not sure," Logan smiled as he listened, the same babbling that had first attracted him to her. "I can't sleep, too much going on in my brain, but I've made a decision."

"That sounds promising. Am I a part of the decision?" He held her hand and pulled her toward him, sliding over to make room for her under the blanket. "It must be important if you are stalking my bedroom. What did you decide?"

"I've decided to sell the rest of the farm. We sold the acreage last year and the house needs to go next. I won't be able to make any decisions while I'm in this house. It's Griff's house, and he is everywhere I turn. Too many memories, mostly good, but the boys are gone, they don't want to live here, and I don't either."

"Where do you want to go?" Logan asked, curious as to what she would say.

Audrey pulled the blanket over her head and pushed herself toward the foot of the bed, "That's the trouble, I don't know. I just don't know."

CHAPTER 70
Audrey

The following few days both dragged and somehow zipped by. Logan stayed with her and promised he would until her sons came, but after they showed up, he would vamoose to the hotel. Her landline rang constantly but not cell phone calls because she hadn't told anyone her new cell number. Another mistake, she told Logan, because she would have to give it out again.

Their nearest neighbor, Rosemary Sage, called with a suggestion about the funeral home. She had once catered a wedding for the Andrew Slaughter family and suggested that Audrey talk to Slaughter and Sons Funeral Home where she could give Griff a final resting place. Logan offered to help with the funeral arrangements, but Audrey thought it awkward and asked Phyllis to call Mr. Slaughter and make an appointment for the two of them to drop by. Logan drove Audrey to Phyllis' home while he went to the Hunter Inn. They downed four lattes plus a glass of wine before driving to Slaughter and Sons. The sugared coffees left them wired, and the tears flowed again. Audrey was crying for Griff, and Phyllis was crying with guilt over killing him.

They rang the doorbell, and Drew Slaughter met them wearing a fishing vest and cap and had his pole and tackle box sitting by the door. He had recorded their appointment time wrong and was anxious to begin his fishing expedition. He shook their hands and folded his in front of his chest. Audrey thought he looked mortician-ish, except for the fishing pole. "Right this way, Widow Lyons, I am so sorry about Griff. I'm sure he was a fine man," Mr. Slaughter stated. He had a deep voice that conflicted with his short, thin stature.

She didn't consider that Drew Slaughter had the characteristics of a stereotypical mortician, yet he did. He had a kind face with a large nose and a crooked smile that drifted across his face. His voice was soft, and he was polite, and she didn't quite know what to think about him. He was gentle but one of those people who liked to move close, within her comfort zone, and his long arms and lanky body moved him closer than she liked. His left hand was missing a thumb, which she later learned he had lost in a machinery accident as a child. She wondered how he could hold a fishing pole with a missing thumb. He had a fuzzy caterpillar mustache, and she watched it wiggle as he spoke. His eyebrows matched his mustache, but they didn't move. The caterpillar mustache, however, wiggled up and down as he talked or smiled. She felt creepy talking to a caterpillar.

Audrey had called herself a widow in the middle of the night, but she didn't expect anyone else to use it and cringed at the term *Widow Lyons*; it reminded her of an old TV western show or B-rated movie. She wondered if she would be tagged with it forever, as in *Hello, Widow Lyons. Could you call me, Widow Lyons?* It would take time to become accustomed to the moniker, especially since she hated it.

The *Widow Lyons* remark and the sight of Mr. Slaughter ready to go fishing caused Audrey to increase the volume of her sobs to snorts, drowning out his words. Griff wore similar clothing when he fished, and the tackle box also happened to be the same model and color as Griff's. Thankfully, Phyllis took the lead and asked the questions that Audrey needed answers to. What day would be available for Griff's funeral? How much will the casket and funeral cost? What does Audrey have to do? Who takes care of the music?

Griff's death had come so suddenly, but maybe all deaths came suddenly, and the grim discussion with Drew Slaughter did little to ease her pain. She sniffled and wheezed through the entire conversation.

When all Phyllis' questions had been answered, Phyllis and Audrey descended to the basement to view and select a casket, while Drew remained upstairs to write a contract. Maybe she should have let her boys pick the casket. They hadn't arrived yet, and she didn't know if they would have an opinion. Their anger about Logan had not abated and anything she did would cause a battle, and she didn't need more stress.

Tears continued to fall as she wandered around the large room, in awe of the available caskets, looking at and poking the pillows of each casket. Made of metal or wood or a combination, they displayed an array of colors spanning the entire color pallet. They had prices posted on them and seemed expensive. Griff would probably grumble about the cost, but she couldn't put him in a cardboard box. He probably would have directed her to check another source. Not Craigslist, but perhaps Amazon.

"This one seems nice and soft," Audrey sobbed out as she stood in front of a royal blue metal casket. "Griff liked a soft bed and it's a pretty blue like the Navy."

Phyllis followed her over to the royal blue casket and opened and closed the lid a few times and asked firmly, "Do you want me to test it for you? You don't buy a car without test driving it, so we should test drive this coffin, as well." She opened the foot panel and pitched herself into it. She lay prone, with her eyes shut and arms neatly folded across her chest and said, "How do I look?" Audrey couldn't help but laugh, but in a few seconds her sobs returned.

"We want to be sure that Griff is comfortable," Phyllis told her as she crawled out of the casket, "It's fine, Audrey, soft and comfortable."

CHAPTER 71
Audrey

Audrey and Griff's sons and families had arrived in Hunter the day before Griff's wake. Everyone in the family knew about Griff's allergy to bee stings, but no one had put together the severity of the stings, and Griff had stubbornly refused to see an allergist for testing. Jeff said, "Isn't it odd that he went fishing so many times and never was stung by a bee?" They knew Griff was obstinate, but to refuse an EpiPen when he was so allergic seemed reckless.

Audrey wanted to make sure that Griff looked his best and dressed herself early. "Mom," said Jeff, "I can go with you. This might be hard to do. You haven't seen him since he died."

"No, I want to do this myself. I want to make sure he looks his best, and I have a tie clip that I'll put on his shirt. He used to wear a tie clip when he dressed up," she told him. Mustering up her strength, she said, "There are some things I have to do by myself."

Logan offered to accompany her to Slaughters, but she insisted that he lay low, not wanting to rally the gossip mongers, specifically Carlee, plus rile her sons and their families. She felt remorse at not being with Griff in the days before he died, especially since she had been enjoying time with Logan.

Audrey had cried off and on all week and hoped the tears had dried up, but she couldn't be sure. Mr. Slaughter met her at the door and escorted her into the viewing room where Griff lay. Audrey pinned the tie clip on his shirt, and the tears welled up in her eyes again.

Mr. Slaughter said, "Audrey, how nice to see you again. Not under these circumstances, of course. I'm sure you must be upset." He was dressed in a dark gray suit, and his eyes smiled as he greeted her. He wore a boutonnière in his lapel and handed her a large pink and green orchid corsage, which he pinned on the front of her dress saying, "This is for you, Audrey."

Audrey answered, "The corsage is nice, thank you. Yes, it is upsetting. You know, Griff and I were married for a long time, and I miss him so. He could be a rascal, but nobody else was like Griff." She teared up again, and her hand started shaking. "I'm sorry, Mr. Slaughter, I can't stop crying."

Drew Slaughter reached for her hand and massaged it. The thumbless hand was weird, but she didn't say anything. "Call me Drew. Would you like a little glass of wine? It might calm you down. Viewings of a loved one can be difficult, and people sometimes say or do foolish things, not realizing the consequences for the family. Wakes can be more difficult than funerals, just for that reason. And I want to alert you that, occasionally, the deceased makes little grunts, usually inaudible, or you could see a slight tremor or a twitch. So far, Griff hasn't twitched, but it's not uncommon and could happen as the body relaxes and gasses are released."

Audrey's eyes grew large, and she gasped and sputtered aloud, "Yes, please, a glass of wine, please, Mr. Slaughter, I mean Drew. Thank you. I should have brought some beverages for people who are coming. Griff would have liked that, except he'd prefer beer. Pale ale was his favorite. Should I call my sons and have them buy some wine before people arrive?"

"No, it isn't necessary. Some people bring drinks, others don't. I don't have a rule about it, and visitors sometimes bring a bottle or two of wine. It happens," Drew said. "I have openers and a few plastic glasses."

Drew and Audrey went into his office and he closed the door. "We shouldn't have any interruptions, and you can drink this in peace and calm yourself." He opened a cupboard and brought out a box of red wine. He looked up and down in the cupboard, dragging out two green coffee mugs, labeled *Slaughter's Funeral Home: Leave the rest to us.* "Oops, it looks like I don't have any glasses, so mugs will have to do." He decanted the wine into the mugs, clean, but faded. "When my wife was alive, she kept a supply of glasses in here, but some were broken at a wake last week. It became a little rowdy, so I'll need to buy some new ones."

Audrey nodded, unsure of what to say.

"I'm not sure if this is proper, but before anyone else arrives, I want to ask you, that is, tell you…uh…that I'd like to see you again, you know, go to dinner or something, after the funeral, that is. You are charming and pretty, and I'd like to know you better. I am aware that the timing is horrible to ask you for a date on the day of your husband's viewing, but I'm afraid someone will snatch you up quickly. Quality women are difficult to find these days."

As he talked, she watched the caterpillar wiggle, thinking it would take off at any moment, but when he stopped talking, the caterpillar ceased to move. She was mesmerized by the caterpillar, wondering if he would brush it off, and only half listened to what he was saying. Suddenly, Drew picked up Audrey's hand and began rubbing it again. Luckily, it was his right hand, so she didn't have to deal with his lack of a thumb.

She snapped back to life, and once she began listening again, she asked, "Mrs. Slaughter is dead? How did she die? I knew her well as we both were avid readers and used the library." She pulled her hand back from his grasp.

"She's been gone quite some time now, four months, I think. It was sudden and tragic, unbelievable, really. She talked about having long, flowing locks and decided to try hair extensions because her hair didn't grow fast. A few days after the extensions had been glued in, she developed a bad headache, maybe a migraine, but we didn't think anything about it. Three days later she died in her sleep. The doctors attributed it to a severe allergy to the glue they used," Drew clarified, shaking his head. "It was terrible, tragic."

"That's awful. Griff died from an allergic reaction to a wasp, and I'm only now realizing that Griff is gone, gone for good," she said, blinking to keep the tears from returning.

Drew picked up her hand again, "Think about it."

"Think about what?" Audrey asked, perplexed.

Drew said, "Dinner. Having dinner with me after things return to normal."

She was stunned and didn't answer. She wasn't sure about eating dinner with a caterpillar or if he'd mind if she invited Logan, too. She liked Logan a lot better than caterpillar man.

They heard some voices as the exterior door in the mortuary closed, and she drank one last swig of wine. "I guess this is it," she said. *Showtime*, the same word Logan had used a few days before.

Still holding her hand, Drew pulled Audrey toward him, caressed her face, and kissed her gently on the cheek. "I'll call you soon, Audrey, real soon."

Audrey thought this was creepy, definitely creepy. Where was Logan when she needed him?

CHAPTER 72
Phyllis

People wandered in and out of the funeral home and quietly visited with each other in small groups. Audrey knew most of the visitors and greeted them all, having cried buckets of tears away during the past week. Everybody hugged her and told her how sorry they were, and if she needed help to please call. Audrey had offers coming out her ears, but she thanked them and nodded and hugged them again.

Audrey's family arrived. Lizzy and Abby wanted the grandchildren to attend the funeral, but not the wake. They all hugged Audrey, and Abby commented, "He looks so peaceful and happy. I can't believe he's gone. He was a force to reckon with, and now he's not."

Friends poured into the chapel, and soon an impromptu bar emerged in the back of the room and people were enjoying themselves. Carlee and Steve arrived last and Carlee was dressed to the nines in a black mesh frilled mini dress with black stockings and strappy heels. The clingy garment left little to the imagination and heads turned. The room grew silent as she strolled through the door. Despite her love of wine and other alcoholic beverages, Carlee maintained her girlish figure. This dress covered her wrinkled neck and arms, and she looked youthful and provocative. She gripped Steve's arm to maintain her balance in her high heels and alcohol-induced state. Steve, dressed in a tux, also cut a handsome figure, although not as provocative as Carlee.

Steve embraced Audrey and held her for a long time, and said, "I've missed you, Audrey, I'll call you soon." With two offers of calls in twenty minutes, the Widow Lyons was overwhelmed.

Gus, in recovery from his ablation, arrived in a wheelchair, gazed at Carlee and sucked in an extra mouthful of air, causing him to cough uncontrollably. With her curvy figure, she was sexier than other women her age, even with the wrinkles. He wheeled himself toward her, "Hello Steve, hello, Carlee. You two are ooh-la-la tonight. I didn't realize this was a formal affair."

"Steve and I wanted to dress up to say bon voyage to Griff properly. You and he looked for babes on the cruise, but never found any because it was a geezer cruise, but I'm positive Griff would like this dress. What do you think, Gussy, would he like it?" Her words were unsteady and slurred as she ran her hands over the front of her dress.

"Oh, yeah, Griff would like it, and I definitely like it. You're the babe tonight," Gus purred. "If you move too close, Griff might sit up and take notice, so stay a few feet away, Carlee, because we don't want to wake up the dead."

"Well, watch this," Carlee said, as she leaned over to kiss Griff on the forehead, which made her dress slink upward, exposing her sweet cheeks covered by black pantyhose. "I'll miss you, Griffy," she slurred. She wobbled and began to lose her balance, and Steve grabbed at her and missed, causing both of them to plunk down on the casket. Griff was a large man and adding the weight of two more people collapsed the bier bouncing Griff to the floor. Horrified, Steve clutched the side of the casket, trying to keep it from falling, but fell to his knees. As he tried to catch himself, he did not notice that his cell phone slid into the casket.

Phyllis screamed, "Mike, Jeff! Somebody, help him," as the funeral director, Mike, and Jeff dashed toward the casket and held it while Drew cranked the bier upward and repositioned Griff. Mike and Jeff then sprang forward to help Carlee and Steve to their feet.

Audrey shrieked again and collapsed to the floor. Drew yanked the pillow from underneath Griff's head and shoved it under her head whispering, "Stay calm, dear Audrey, I'll find you a cup of wine from my office."

Mike and Jeff glowered at Mr. Slaughter cradling their mom's head, "What the...?"

CHAPTER 73
Audrey

Audrey had dreaded this day and knew that her life would change. It had already changed, losing her husband and the father of her children, she felt truly alone. And the funeral would make things final. She had a lot to learn about being the Widow Lyons, but one thing was sure, life would be different without Griff. And with Logan, if that's what she decided.

Audrey expected three hundred people at the service to bid Griff a bon voyage. He and Audrey had lived in Hunter nearly all their lives, had been active in community organizations, and had many friends. The funeral was next on the agenda, and she was grateful that Phyllis had dealt with all of the details, including the flowers, music, obituary, and speakers. All Audrey had to do was hold herself together.

A steady stream of friends and neighbors had deposited an enormous cache of food in Audrey's kitchen; casseroles, vegetable dishes, baked goods, and bottles of wine. Her sons and their families sorted through the array and ate some and froze some. As friends dropped by, Audrey joined the munchers, hoping she would be able to fit into her dress for the funeral.

Audrey drove to the mortuary early, planning to greet guests as they passed into the building. Drew met her at the door and escorted her into the main hall where the shiny coffin sat at the front of the church. The lid was closed, and Drew had added silver angels on the four corners of the casket, which made Audrey happy. More tears. *Griff could be an angel*, she thought, not really believing it. He would cause St. Peter more trouble than he knew what to do with. She hesitated as she approached the casket and patted it firmly, embraced and kissed it, saying, "Oh, Griff, I miss you so, what will I do without you?" She sat down on the pew and asked, "Drew, could I have one more look at him, just for a second before everyone arrives, so I can be certain that he's peaceful and not stressed?"

Still gazing at Audrey, Drew nodded and said, "Sure," and unsnapped the cover of the casket.

Audrey stood up and approached the box and screamed, "That's not Griff, that's a woman. Where's Griff?"

Drew jerked his head around and stared at the woman dressed in a turquoise suit and clutching a rosary, lying silent in the coffin. "Oh, no, this is Mrs. Dexter. I must have switched caskets. This navy blue model is popular and lots of people buy it. Her funeral is this afternoon at the Catholic church, which is across town. I'll have to switch the bodies out. What a mess."

Drew grabbed his cell phone from his pocket and hit speed dial, calling his son to remove the casket from the mortuary and load it into the hearse. Audrey heard him say, "With only two of us, Andy, it'll be tough to maneuver Mrs. Dexter into the hearse, but we can do it."

As soon as Andy arrived, the two pushed the bier from behind and Drew guided it toward the hearse. The bier creaked and jumped as they rolled it outside the funeral home. When they exited the building, they trotted toward the hearse when the wheel snagged in small pothole. The casket tumbled to the ground, opened, and spilled Mrs. Dexter to the sidewalk. "Drat! I've been meaning to fix that pothole," Drew grumbled, as they straightened the casket and bier and returned Mrs. Dexter to her bed. Drew brushed the sand and gravel remnants from her clothes. Griff's casket now had a dent in it, but they slammed it shut and sped off to switch the bodies.

Inside the mortuary, Audrey's tear ducts had reopened as their family and friends joined her for Griff's send off. "Where's Dad?" Mike whispered to his mother, "Why isn't the casket here?"

She was sobbing uncontrollably, sputter, sputter, "He went to the Catholic Church and Drew and Andy went to retrieve him."

"Dad's not Catholic, he was Baptist," Mike commented, wrinkling his brow in puzzlement.

Audrey shook her head, "No, we're not Catholic, but they mistakenly brought a Catholic woman instead of Griff."

Griff's service was delayed until Drew and Andy returned with Griff. The guests had been restless, but Mike and Jeff wandered through the aisles apologizing for the delay.

Drew and Andy placed Griff's casket on the bier, and Drew peeked into the casket to verify he hadn't been disheveled and adjusted his hair a bit. He patted him on the chest, and whispered, "I'm sorry, Griff, but everything's all right now."

Audrey sucked in a deep breath and grasped the hands of both her sons, relieved that everything was coming together when a loud pfft-y sound emerged from the direction of the casket. A burp? No, it was a fart. Audrey gasped, and Mike blurted out, "Dad? Is that Dad?"

Audrey grimaced and declared, "Drew told me that sometimes dead people make little noises, but that's a full-bodied fart, like Griff made in the bathroom." Giggles rippled through the audience, and Mike said, loudly enough for the guests to hear, "That's our Dad. What else can happen?"

The *what else* happened a few minutes after the chaplain recited a solemn prayer about Griff's soul arriving to heaven in a timely fashion. As he said "Amen," the Anslem Douglas song, *Who Let the Dogs Out?* roared maximum volume from the casket. Carlee tugged on Steve's sleeve, "Steve, that's your phone. You must have dropped it in the casket." It was on a looped soundtrack and went on for several seconds before Carlee repeated to Steve what she had already said.

"What? It's not mine because I lost my phone," Steve whispered back. He patted his pockets searching for his cell but instead discovered his two hearing aids.

Carlee reiterated her previous statement hissing, "Steve, your phone is ringing from the casket. Take it out of the casket."

Steve wasn't listening and couldn't hear if he were, looked at her uncomprehendingly, as if to say, "Who? Me?"

"Carlee rose and stepped to the casket, lifted the foot cover, and looked at Audrey, "Audrey, they forgot Griff's shoes. He's barefoot. They forgot his shoes." The phone continued to ring, as Carlee rummaged through the folds of the casket and found Steve's phone, just as the sound stopped.

Audrey stood and turned her head looking for Drew, "Drew, where are his shoes? Griff needs his shoes. He had a bunion, but he can wear sandals."

Steve opened his flip phone and exclaimed to no one in particular, "It was another damned robocall."

CHAPTER 74
Audrey

Drew had warned Audrey that the graveside service would draw only a small crowd, down from the three hundred attending the funeral service. But the gravesite was jammed with people. The cold air plus a bright warming sunshine made for a perfect day. The sky was sprinkled with large white, puffy clouds and birds passed over the cemetery searching for nesting possibilities in the pines that surrounded the cemetery. The attendees had bundled up and were restless, stamping their feet, trying to stay warm. Drew draped blankets around Audrey and Phyllis, who had been her rock during this time. Phyllis, suffering from guilt about Griff's death, was going out of her way to help Audrey.

The minister said a few words, but Audrey didn't pay much attention because her sole thought was that Griff was gone. A uniformed person handed her a folded flag, and the casket elevator began to clank and groan as they lowered Griff into the ground. Audrey had used up all her tears, but Phyllis hadn't and continued to weep. Without thinking, Phyllis stood up, stepped to the edge of the grave, and leaned over it, sinking her high heels into the dampened soil. Gus didn't know what she was doing, and he moved his wheelchair toward her, grabbing her arm trying to pull her away, but one of her high-heeled shoes slipped off, and she lost her balance. Gus tried to catch her, but instead bumped her into the hole, and she landed on top of the casket.

The crowd came alive with *oohs* and *what happened*, some giggles and some shrieks, and Phyllis squealed, "Get me out of here! Hurry! Somebody, help me!"

Drew and his son stared in awe for a short second before they rallied to stop the elevator. They reversed the direction and the elevator grinded the casket to the surface where Audrey's sons assisted Phyllis to solid ground. The casket swayed a little, and she teetered, but typical of Phyllis, she found it hilarious and began to roar with laughter. Her comical hysteria soon caught on and within seconds, the entire audience, including Audrey and her family, were laughing boisterously. The perfect finish for Griff's funeral. He would have approved.

CHAPTER 75
Phyllis

The crowd began to disperse, and several people asked Phyllis, "Do we need to call the EMTs? You might be hurt."

"No, I'm fine," Phyllis said, "I need to change clothes, but I'm fine."

Steve and Carlee wheeled Gus to their car while their friends Bill and Rosemary hurried from the cemetery to The Purple Fox to set up the reception, and to ready the food they had prepared. Audrey and Phyllis remained behind to greet guests and thank them for coming.

When Rosemary and Bill arrived at The Purple Fox, the door was ajar and the manager stood outside, shivering, smoking, and waiting for the reception to begin. The bartender had already taken his place behind the bar. Rosemary obtained control of the food, shifting her creations from the refrigerators and ovens to a central table easily accessible by the attendees. With such a large crowd at the cemetery, she wondered if she had underestimated the number of people who would be attending and worried that she would run out of food. *Too late now*, she thought.

After all the adventures of the previous three days leading up to Griff's wake followed by a tumble into the grave, Phyllis wanted a stress relief as well as a change of clothes, and they stopped at her house, "This is too much for me."

"Yes, it has been a day to remember. I can't believe he's gone. And if Drew calls me the *Widow Lyons* one more time, I might smack him," Audrey confided to Phyllis.

They went into the house, and Phyllis said, "I'll be just a second, stress relief lies in the bedroom, and I'll change my clothes. Could you bring me a glass and ice? Make that two glasses." Phyllis' emotions had edged out her composure, and she continued to sob, "I might have killed him, Audrey, but I only wanted to help. Everything we did, we did for you. There's an envelope on the table, Griff planned to give it to you. He wanted you to have it, only he died first." Audrey picked up a sealed envelope with her name on it in Griff's scrawled handwriting.

She didn't know what Phyllis was referring to, and thought she was delusional, distraught over falling into the grave. She looked at the envelope. *Something from Griff? I think I should wait to read this in private,* she thought and jammed it in her purse. She poked her head in and saw Phyllis sitting on the bed half dressed, looking lost. "Why do you need ice, Phyllis?"

An unopened bottle of vodka sat on the dresser, and Phyllis focused her eye on it. "I need it, that's all."

The two women sat on the bed, and after the second glass, they slid to the floor where they drank and toasted Griff, grieving about losing him. Soon the bottle was empty, and the two grievers giggled at all the events of the past few days.

Audrey's head was not clear, but she said, "Okay, Phyllis, we either have to go to the liquor store or to The Purple Fox because we are out of vodka, but I'm not done drinking. Rosemary's food will be gone and some of the guests will have left already because it's been over an hour. Let's drink one more itty-bitty tipple-topple, and you can call Tequila or Suzy or whatever the heck her name is. The Uber girl. Better yet, I'll call Logan because he'll be glad to pick us up, meaning we don't have to drive, because it would be a kicker to get a DUI on the way to Griff's bon voyage party."

Audrey was correct, Logan was happy to ferry them from Phyllis and Gus' house to The Purple Fox, although half blotto or possibly more when they arrived at the reception. They had unclear heads and slurred words, and their steps were unsteady, but Logan steadied them with their arms and accompanied them safely into the building. Noise drifted out of the restaurant, and as soon as they entered, guests surrounded them, hugging and offering words of sympathy. Many had already left, but a pile of envelopes sat waiting to be opened.

Lizzy came up from behind and said, "Phyllis? Audrey? Have you had *tee many martoonis?*"

"Me? Noooo…not me. Well, we had a couple drinks, maybe three, but I'm not drunk." Audrey answered. "We might need another soon."

"Four," Phyllis corrected Audrey flatly. "Not *martoonis*, though, vodkas. And they were *delishioshush*. Where's Griff?"

Lizzy said, "Griff? He's not here, you know, we kinda buried him today."

"Oh, yeah, I remember now, I meant Gus," Phyllis answered, "Gus. He's my honeybunch. No one else."

Rosemary came up and said, "What you two need is food and luckily we have plenty. The lasagna is nearly gone, but no one ate the deviled eggs or cheesecake rolls. I'll bring you each a plate of food."

Carlee, surprisingly sober, leaned over and whispered, "Don't eat the cheesecake rolls, unless you like blue cheese. They taste like she used blue cheese instead of cream cheese, and the deviled eggs have cayenne pepper on top that will blow your top off. Clearly, this is not Rosemary's best showing."

"Who cares, Carlee? Griff surely wouldn't."

CHAPTER 76
Audrey

Logan wanted to lay low for the next few days, but Audrey had other thoughts. Jeff and Mike and Ethan pulled out the fishing tackle and camping gear to spend a couple days in search of fish, and Abby and Lizzy went to Pocatello to do some shopping, taking the three girls. Abby and Lizzy wanted Audrey to go with them, and tried to ply her with spa time, but she refused. She had received an insurance check for the lost skis and clothing, cashed it, and gave them the money to try to replicate the stolen items.

"Go, please, leave me in peace. I need solace," she said.

Abby teased, "No, Audrey, you need a different five letter word: Logan. Call him up and do something fun with him. Your BFF status is going to be sorely diminished if you don't have some Logan time."

Audrey blushed, and Lizzy agreed. Emma, Sophie, and Ava taunted her with a chant, "Lo-Gan, Lo-Gan, Lo-Gan."

As soon as they left, Audrey called Logan, "Everybody's gone, so why don't you come out, and we can figure out what's in my future."

"You mean our future, don't you? We're going to be together, aren't we?" Logan wrinkled his brow, hoping that their future would be together, but he knew she was grieving and probably needed more time. It had taken him a full two years to figure out how to live without Joan, but he didn't want to wait two years, that was definitely too long.

He arrived in record time with a bouquet of long-stemmed roses and two milkshakes in hand. "I've never known you not to want ice cream, and these looked good to me. Do you want strawberry or mint chocolate chip?"

"Both," she said as she snatched them both from him, sucking first on one straw followed by the other.

Logan sighed, "I should have brought three. So, what are we talking about today, Audrey, your future? Or mine? Or both of us?"

"Do you remember that Steven King book *Shawshank Redemption* and the line about getting busy living or getting busy dying? I've been thinking about that book all week and have decided that I want to get busy living. I loved Griff once, and he loved me, but he's gone, that relationship is over, and it's time to move on. I fell in love with you slowly, but now it's like I'm on speed dial, I'm ready to live. I finished reading a book on grief this week, wondering how to deal with Griff's sudden death, and it suggested not to make any decisions for one or two years, but you're seventy and I'm sixty-seven. We can't wait, and if you're serious, we can move forward but, Logan, in the meantime we have a lot of stuff to do and hurdles to overcome and we are almost out of time."

CHAPTER 77
Audrey

The sun came out, hallelujah. Sun and no wind and a few wispy clouds. Since the day of the funeral, Hunter had been clouded over with drizzles of rain, day after day. Not enough rain to help with planting, Audrey thought, but enough to make it a messy day. But today was a heavenly day. Audrey hadn't been to the cemetery all week and thought it was a good time to go. She missed Griff and thought it would be proper to check on him. Mike and Jeff ordered a headstone for Griff and had it engraved with his name and the words *The Fish Are Now Safe*, but it had not yet arrived.

She stopped at the local drive-through and bought a double cheeseburger, which was Griff's all-time favorite food. She ordered it protein style, no bun, which Griff never would have done. She loaded it with condiments and headed to the cemetery. "I'll have lunch with Griff," she said offhandedly, hoping he wouldn't think she was gloating about her having a cheeseburger and him not.

Today when she arrived, the cemetery was vacant, not a vehicle in sight, and it was silent, so silent. With no wind, it was as silent as a graveyard, oh yeah it was a graveyard. Someone had visited and left some coins, maybe about thirty or forty cents in a plastic bowl at the top of the grave. She wondered why someone left the coins but then vaguely remembered something about coins and graves when Griff was in the military. She'd have to look it up on Google, since Google knows everything.

Audrey finished her burger and frowned as she noticed the runny condiments had dripped onto her blouse and pants and opened her purse for tissues or napkins to blot them off. The envelope that Phyllis had given her tumbled out to the grass. "Now is just as good a time as any," Audrey said, as she sat down on a nearby bench and opened the envelope. It was a letter from Griff. At first, she thought it was a love letter because Griff had drawn hearts on the top and bottom which was odd because Griff had never written her even a postcard and didn't draw either.

Dear Audrey,

I just finished Phyllis' romance school and am now romantic.

I love you, but I'm going to give you to Logan because I love someone else, too.

Love, your husband, Griff

What the heck? Did Griff love someone else? He was giving me to Logan? Pure Griff. It's a good thing he's dead, or I'd kill him, she laughed.

She was ready to leave when she heard some noise, people talking. The sounds started low and grew louder, but not loud enough for her to decipher the words. In fact, they didn't sound like words at all, more of rustling or rumbling with some swishing thrown in for good behavior. She felt alone, and saw no one, yet she felt, and even weirder, she smelled Griff, the strong soap that he used after he had been on the tractor all day. It was if he were standing right next to her, almost, but not quite, touching her.

The wind picked up and began to curl around her, and she felt a tickle float around her hair, on her ears and the nape of her neck, but the trees stood motionless. The wind had not touched them. The movement startled her, and she swept it aside, it returned, and she shooed it away again. She knew in her brain that Griff was six feet down, but she lurched when she heard a sound, half chuckle and half growl, she had heard many times before, and the soap smell intensified. "Griff? Are you there?" Audrey said, knowing that the wind or her brain was playing tricks. She rotated three hundred and sixty degrees, but she was alone. She heard his chuckle one more time, and the serenity and silence returned. No wind, no tickles, no chuckles, and no soap, just calm. She felt at peace, and Logan was waiting.

She stood for a few minutes awaiting Griff's reappearance, but he had vanished for good. She ran to her car and drove the shortest route to the hotel where Logan had been staying for the past two weeks.

Using the extra key card that he had given to her, she burst into Logan's room, and he looked up from the book he was reading. She was out of breath, but her words came out just as she meant them to for a change. "I saw Griff. At the cemetery. He gave me to you. Do you still want me?"

Acknowledgments

Thank you, Tom, for believing in me during our 53.8 years together, encouraging me by insisting that I could do anything. Without your support, so much that we did and enjoyed together would not have happened. Semper fi, Marine! I'm missing you already!

This series was given birth by my daughter Elizabeth and my editor Anna who both told me to write a romance novel, but not being a romantic person, I laughed because I'm much too old for the bare-necked and bare-chested romance novels that lie on the library shelves. They told me I was thinking wrong, and that I needed to write what I know and to write a romance series for people over seventy. Since Tom had told me I could do anything, I said, *why not*, and they said *go for it*, and here they are. Wrinkly Bits.

Thank you, to my editors, AnnaMarie McHargue and Anita Stephens, *Words With Sisters*, without your talent and time, I would still be floundering, as I continue to do most days.

Thank you, Linda Alden, for your tireless interest and assistance each time I got stuck. The four o'clock wine time helped, too.

Thank you to the many seniors who are involved in romantic hijinks, several of whom are my long-time friends. You gave me fodder for this series. I could name names but would not embarrass you for the world. Enjoy the journey!

Thank you to my Facebook followers for reading my bi-weekly blog, *Wrinkly Bits* or *Wrinklybits.com*. Writing can be a lonely process and receiving your comments and feedback encourages me and keeps me going.

Thank you to Elizabeth and Chris Hume and Cole and Pam Cushman for your continued support for also giving me grandchildren to spoil. Nate, Tommy, Roe, Maggie: You brighten my day, every day!

I hope you enjoy my stories as much as I enjoy writing them.

About the Author

My husband often teased that I had two useless degrees, a B.S. and an M.A., both in Sociology, along with a quite a few classes in Psychology, but he was wrong. Those degrees made me a master of people-watching and now with twenty cruises and a lifetime of doing what I do best, I have observed more senior hijinks than I can possibly remember. I taught composition for eleven years and spent three years as a Marine Corps Officer. Retired, I spend my time writing, and currently author a bi-weekly blog "Wrinkly Bits" available at Wrinklybits.com. Age is only a number, get on with living.